Justin McCarthy

My Enemy's Daughter

A novel. Vol. 1

Justin McCarthy

My Enemy's Daughter
A novel. Vol. 1

ISBN/EAN: 9783337213657

Printed in Europe, USA, Canada, Australia, Japan

Cover: Foto ©Andreas Hilbeck / pixelio.de

More available books at **www.hansebooks.com**

MY ENEMY'S DAUGHTER.

LONDON:
ROBSON AND SONS, PRINTERS, PANCRAS ROAD, N.W.

MY ENEMY'S DAUGHTER.

A Novel.

By JUSTIN M^CCARTHY,

AUTHOR OF " PAUL MASSIE," "THE WATERDALE NEIGHBOURS," ETC.

IN THREE VOLUMES.

VOL. I.

LONDON:

TINSLEY BROTHERS, 18 CATHERINE ST., STRAND.

1869.

CONTENTS OF VOL. I.

MY ENEMY'S DAUGHTER.

CHAPTER I.

RETROSPECT; AND MIST.

IT is a wet Sunday evening in the leaden heart of London. I am now in the Bloomsbury region; and perhaps I need hardly say that nothing on earth could be more dull, dingy, and unpicturesque in itself than the prospect from my windows. Yet just now, in the deepening gloom of a rainy dusk, I seem to look on something not unlike one of the most picturesque and romantic scenes whereon my eyes have ever rested. "Ich weiss nicht was soll es bedeuten;" but the ridges of the houses opposite begin to show through the steaming mist fantastically like the outlines of the hills I used to see every day years ago, and the broad blank lying between me and over the way may

easily enough seem filled by the stretch of bay
I have watched when it lay wild and drear on
the wet evenings of late autumn like this. The
kindly, loving, artistic fog and rain, which now
hide all but the faint and softened outlines of our
street, have done this for me; and lo! in Bloomsbury I am looking upon sea and hill once more.
The very sounds of London city-life come to help
out the illusion. That cry of the oysterman below is a good deal more like the scream of some
sea-bird than most theatrical imitations are like
the reality. The church-bells clinking and toll-
ing for evening service are to me now the bell of
the church to which I used to be conducted when
a boy on Sundays, and with which so many of the
associations of my after-life inevitably connect
themselves. It used to be a dreadful ceremonial,
that service, to us boys, on the fine Sundays of
summer. It was bad enough in winter; but in
summer it became unspeakably more torturing.
There was a window in the church close to where
we used to sit—poor little weary, yawning mar-
tyrs—and the branches of an elm flapped unceas-
ingly on the panes. Tantalus-torture was it to
watch the tender, lucent leaves, free in the glo-

rious air of May or June, as they flickered across
the window, and seemed to whisper of the blue
sky and the shingly strand and the waves of tran-
sparent emerald which they could see and we
could not; while the organ pealed and the clergyman preached the long sermon to which we never
listened. I do not know how it is, that when I
thus sit alone of nights and do not feel inclined
to read, or steadily to go to work at something,
every object I see, flame, cloud, or even chimney-
pot, reminds me in an indescribable, irresistible
way, of some object belonging to the dear dull
little seaport town where I, Emanuel Temple
Banks, was born some five-and-thirty years ago.

I have now written my full name, but it is
long since I have been known otherwise than as
Emanuel Temple. I pruned my name down to
its present brevity for reasons which shall be ex-
plained in due time. I was called "Emanuel
Temple" because my mother had a proper wo-
manly objection to commonplace or vulgar names,
and since we could call ourselves nothing better
than Banks, resolved that we should at least have
euphonious and elegant Christian names. Therefore, instead of becoming, as was suggested, John

Banks and Peter Banks, my brother and I became
Emanuel Temple Banks and Theodore Eustace
Banks respectively. I scarcely know by what process Theodore Eustace and myself were brought
up. We were the only children—I the elder by
a year—and my father died when I was six years
old. He had owned fishing-boats, and was doing
well, until, at the instigation of my mother, he
unfortunately took to immature building speculations, and failed accordingly, fishing-boats and
all going down in the land-wreck. Indeed, my
poor father did not remain long after the ruin of
his venture, and my mother had to live by making gloves and trying to let lodgings. She had
been a genteel woman of her class at one time;
and being engaged in one of the few pretentious
millinery shops in our little town, was regarded
by her friends as having made quite a sort of
mésalliance when she married my father, who was
then only a good-looking young boat-builder, with
a fine voice for singing. She was very sentimental then, was poor mother—so she has often told
me—and those were the days when the heart of
sentimental womanhood was divided between the
Corsair and the *Lady of the Lake*. My mother

loved both, but leaned to the *Corsair;* and found a resemblance between that hero and my father. To her latest days she was fond of repeating whole strings of "My own Medora," and Ellen and James Fitzjames—and I doubt much whether *Locksley Hall* and *Maud* are often recited and raved about and glorified in the shops of provincial milliners just now. Poetry and romance seem to have taken a terrible grip of the female heart at that time, and to have released the squeeze in our days.

Besides being romantic, my mother was likewise religious—a combination which also does not seem to flourish in our time. Heaven only knows how painfully she laboured and strove to give and get us some education in religion and poetry. She loved her sons dearly, weakly, and her most passionate prayer of nights was that they might never, never leave her. The dearest wish and ambition of her heart would have been that one of the two might become a gentle clergyman, and the other, whatever his ordinary pursuits, a churchwarden. If she had lived until now, O what a Ritualist she would have been! Her prayers for the future of her sons were not even half granted. One of the sons went, very young, to America, and became a Rationalist. The other came up to London and turned opera-singer.

As soon as I could write a decent hand, some good-natured person got me a situation in the office of an attorney and land-agent. I began as the youngest and lowest of clerks—a sort of cross between a messenger and a scrivener's apprentice —never, of course, intended to develop into that pretentious grub the articled clerk, who in his time develops into the attorney. I had five shillings a-week to begin with, and I think the head clerk had a hundred and fifty pounds a-year. Perhaps, but for subsequent events, I might have worked up to hold that position, and receive that emolument, in my turn. Indeed, I mounted very steadily up to thirty shillings a-week, but there I stopped and got off the ladder. Before I had attained that eminence, however, my brother, who had tried one or two situations unsuccessfully, and was always alarming my mother with his longing and projects for going to sea, compromised matters by resolving to seek his fortune in America. My mother had to consent at last—indeed, hard times allowed her no choice—and some poor outfit was scraped together. It was arranged that I must stay at home and work for mother until her sons should become wealthy men, when we were to live in one country and one home, and she was to keep house for both. We had much crying and feeble keeping-up of each other's spirits, and we parted full of grief, but not without hope. Theodore Eustace took with him the latch-key of our door, with which he used to let himself in of nights, promising himself and us that he would return before long, laden, doubtless, with wealth, arrive unexpectedly, and opening the door softly, steal in upon my mother and me as we sate some evening by the fire and talked of him.

He wrote to us when he got a situation in a dry-goods store, Broadway, New York, and very soon after, when he lost it; when he went out next and became successively a hawker, a railway-clerk, a photographer, an electro-biologist, a newspaper correspondent, and a farmer. In each successive calling he was most positively to succeed, and to make up for all the time—never very much, that was one comfort—which he had lost in the

vocation just abandoned. He never remitted anything except a sketch of a forest clearing, and a
dried musquito as a specimen of the animal life
of the New World. I think my mother placed
the musquito's corpse tenderly in her bosom.
He has sown all his wild oats long since. He
was lately married for the third time, and I believe got money, or property of some sort, with
each of the wives. He was just the sort of bright,
exuberant, reckless, blundering, soft-hearted fellow whom a certain kind of women, and all dogs,
and all animals of tender natures indeed, instinc-
tively take to. He has many children, and is
well-to-do now and steady. He still writes, although at long intervals. He says he has the
latch-key still, which I doubt—Theodore Eustace
was seldom very literal in his statements. But
even if he has, it will never open the door for
which he meant to use it. Were he to return to
our old street, so sunny and pleasant in summer,
with its glimpse of the sea through every lane, he
would find no creature there whom once he knew;
and the place itself would know him no more.
The little row of houses in which we lived has
been pulled down long since to make way for

more pretentious habitations—marine residences, semi-detached villas, sea-side boarding-houses, and the like. In my own season of success I often contemplated a tour through America as a "star." I thought of setting New York wild with admiration, filling my brother's heart with ecstasy, and cramming his house with presents. Something, however, always intervened to postpone the journey, and before I had finally made up my mind, the best of my voice had gone, and my reputation was pulled down, like our old house, to make way for a new erection upon a more secure basis.

From my father I had inherited a good voice, *et præterea nil.* There are families through which a good voice appears to move in order of primogeniture; and I have observed that a fine tenor, thus bequeathed, rarely seems an inheritance which brings much worldly providence or prosperity. My father was always under the impression that he only wanted a lucky chance to have made him another Incledon, who was of course his hero, and whose rolling, quavering, florid style, unknown to this generation, he did his best to imitate. I cannot help thinking the

fishing-boats and the building speculations would
have fared a good deal better if my father had had
no more voice than a grasshopper, and had therefore found no admiring idlers to persuade him
that he was another Incledon. However, it is
quite certain that at an early age my voice became
remarkable; and some of my father's whilom admiring idlers did generously take me in hand
and provide me with not very inadequate training. My mother's dread of my developing power
was turned into confidence and pride when I began to sing in the choir of our church on Sundays. I paused not in my progress until I had
actually been promoted to the post of *primo
tenore* there, at a remuneration of twenty pounds
a-year.

This seemed to us what sea-coast people call
"the third wave" of promise, on which we were
to be safely lifted into prosperity. But it came
a little too late. My mother's life had long been
on the wane. Grief, anxiety, poverty, late long
sewing, had been doing for years their combined
best with her, and at last she utterly broke down.
I was nineteen years old when I found myself
watching, in the gray of a cold spring morning,

with our clergyman and one or two kindly old
women, by the side of the bed in which my
mother recovered at last from all sickness and
all sorrow. A pale, wan ray of the rising sun
gleamed upon the cold face whereon so little of
the sunshine of happiness had rested. A quaint
little burial-ground clings and straggles along the
side of one of the hills which rises over the
bay. You may count every tombstone and grave-
hillock from the deck of any of the fishing-boats
that toss in the surf beneath. Many a monu-
ment is erected there by the widow of some lost
skipper or mate in memory of the husband whose
bones have been tossed ashore on some Pacific
island, or have been gnawed and mumbled by the
Arctic bear. There we laid my mother, disturb-
ing for the purpose some of the ashes which had
been coffined when my father was buried. I came
away from the grave alone. The scene I saw as
I turned away is before me now. I see it clearly
— as clearly as then. The hills — we used to
think them mountains—that embraced the long
narrow stretch of bay in their arms; the far line
of the horizon; the straggling white town just
under my feet; the strand whereon lay the

hauled-up fishing-boats; the merchant-brigs and
the coal-schooners anchored; the one war-sloop;
the tree-tufted summit of one hill, conspicuous
among its bare and bald companions; and over
all the gray sky breaking faintly into sunlight—
as over my own life the mist of sadness and
loneliness just breaking a little with the purple
light of youth.

I am not going to write of my grief and loneliness. I suffered bitterly and heavily, but the
passing away of a year or so softened the grief
into a gentle memory. At twenty I was full of
hope and spirits again, secretly perhaps even
proud of my desolate independence, and believ-
ing myself a personage of rare endowments, destined to some special and wonderful career. But
because of my mother's death, and other and
earlier associations too, the gray days of spring
have always worn for me the most melancholy
and dispiriting aspect. I see the early spring,
not in budding brightness, and beauty, and hope,
as poetical people tell me they see it, but dim,
dreary, boding, suggestive of loneliness, associated with partings, graves, and death.

CHAPTER II.

I was, then, an attorney's clerk all the week-
days up to five or six o'clock, and a singer of
sacred music every Sunday,—a singer in that
same little church the sermons and the bough-
shaded windows of which used to distract me so
when a boy.

I was growing a sort of little celebrity in our
small town because of my voice and my supposed
musical genius. I mean that I was getting to
be known among all that small middle class
whose highest reach towards society was the patronage of the clergyman's wife or the attorney
and his family. Our town was divided morally,
and indeed one might say geographically, into
three sections. There were "the townspeople,"
—ourselves,—who lived in the streets on what
I may call the middle terrace of the ascent on
which chance had placed us. We were all tra-

ders, shopkeepers, clerks, master carpenters, a few engineers, two or three teachers of French and music, a good many principals of small English schools, a good many civil servants of the unpretending class. Beneath us stretched, reaching to the water's edge, and straggling away rather towards the rising sun, a lower plateau of population, consisting of publichouse-keepers, rope-makers, block-makers, fishermen, sailors, and nondescript poor people of all kinds—poor people avowing and indeed going in for pauperism. Above us, and stretching away westward, were the villas and mansions of the gentry, the swells who only came into the town to buy at the shops, or to reach the sea. Of these it is enough to say—for this story has little to do with the aristocracy of the earth—that a nobleman who owned nearly all the country round and half the town was the apex of the pyramid, and the base was formed by the fashionable doctor of our district, the attorney in whose office I worked, two or three clergymen, the collectors of customs and excise, and a few retired naval officers. Now these three sections were each a world to itself. Nobody on the higher plateau knew anything about us except as people who made things or had things to sell; we knew little of the lower plateau except in an equally general sort of way. Therefore when I say that I was becoming a sort of small celebrity, I mean of course only in my own middle sphere. The gentlemen and ladies above knew and cared just as much about me and my like as the tarry lads of the lower town did, or indeed as the crabs and star-fish on the beach might have done. If any grand personage or grand personage's wife had been attracted by my singing at church some day, and had been good enough to ask the clergyman who the singer was, the answer would have been, "Only a young man from the town," and that would have settled the matter. That was enough to know; that was all anybody could want to know.

But I was getting to be talked about among people of my own world. I used to be invited out to small evening parties, where, lonely as I was,—and at this period having reached the cynical stage, and being professedly scornful of earth's joys,—I went very delightedly. I bought kid-gloves, and wore my collar turned down. Those were not days when even a musical aspirant could

venture upon a moustache in a town like ours, or
I doubt not that I would have wrestled with Nature to extract by unknown philtres and essences
the precious ornament from her gift. Of course
I was a good deal vain of my voice and my personal appearance. Kind heaven, which had taken
from me so much that was dear, had left me
youth's delicious consolation—vanity. Had I not
been such a self-conceited ass just then, I must
needs have been very unhappy.

We used to practise—we did not call it "re-
hearsing"—three or four times a week in the
choir of the church, the organist being intrusted
with the keys for the purpose. "We" were generally four. First was Miss Griffin the organist,
who could sometimes pipe a flat and feeble note
of her own. Miss Griffin was a spinster fast falling into years—nay, it seemed to me then quite
stricken in years, although I know now that she
could not have been far past thirty. But she was
very old-maidenish in appearance, with dull hair
done into old-fashioned spiral ringlets : a sharp-
nosed and perhaps frosty, but withal very kindly,
little dowdy. Next in years—but with such an
interval!—came our bass,—a stout young fellow,

son of a master carpenter. Then came the tenor, Emanuel Temple Banks; and last came the soprano, a girl of German parentage and birth, Christina Braun.

Christina, I should think, was then just a little younger than myself. She was the daughter of a German toy-maker, who—half-mechanist, half-artist, whole dreamer—had striven to make and sell playthings of a new kind, with a scientific, philosophical, and moral purpose about them, for the æsthetical entertainment and culture of children. The philosophical toy-maker did not succeed in winning much of the sympathy of our town for his refined and lofty purpose. He failed altogether, became bankrupt, gave up all struggle thenceforward, and resigned the conduct of exist· ence into the hands of his daughter, who sang in churches and chapels and elsewhere for the means of living.

I used to think Christina a wonderful young person because she had been born in Germany, and could speak German. She had at this time been many years in England, and must have been quite a child when she left her native country. We used to pronounce her name as if it were similar in sound with the name of the familiar substance sold in pork-shops. Being at this time of my life still rather shy so far as girls were concerned, I knew little or nothing of Miss Braun for months and months, but that she had a strong voice and fine eyes, and that she had a happy capacity for talking freely enough when anyone chose to speak, and remaining contentedly silent when no one did so choose. She was a remarkable girl to look at. She had a great fleece of fair hair thrown back off her forehead, and only kept up in some way or other from falling about her shoulders and waist, which indeed it did more than once in the choir, to the great annoyance and scandal of Miss Griffin, who, I think, by the look that came into her eyes, always regarded this little mischance as a pure piece of coquetry. Christina had beautiful deep-shining eyes, dark-gray in colour—much darker indeed than the tinge of her hair would have led one to expect. She had a bright complexion and a rather large mouth, from which issued when she sang a strange and almost startling voice: we used to consider it somewhat coarse. I don't think I thought her a handsome girl; I rather fancy she seemed to me all hair and eyes. But I have hardly any distinct impression of our earliest meetings, and I positively cannot by any effort of memory recall my first sight of one who afterwards exercised such an influence over my life, and whom I once so deeply loved. There is no mystery about the story I purpose to tell, and I make known at once that everything in my existence which is worth recording is in some way associated with the memory of Christina Braun.

We four, then—Miss Griffin, our basso, Christina, and I—used to foregather in the church-choir of evenings ; and after having practised as we considered long enough, would very often conclude by going to Miss Griffin's to tea, and there compensating ourselves with the newest operatic pieces for our enforced devotion to sacred music. Miss Griffin and her mamma taught music, and some of their pupils used to help us out occasionally with duets, trios, choruses, and the like. I remember nothing particular about the mamma, except that she was an odd, vivacious, flighty little old personage, who could speak French. I don't know why she considered it proper always to address Christina Braun in French, or why she assumed that a German girl must necessarily be able to understand that language. But she always did so. "*Eh bien*, Christina, *chère petite*," was her usual greeting; and during the course of any conversation, if she had occasion to address a word to the tall and plump *chère petite*, Mrs. Griffin always lapsed into French, and Christina, with perfect docility and gravity, as regularly replied in the same tongue, which she seemed to speak with fluency.

Sometimes I was the only gentleman among all these ladies; and this, perhaps, may partly account for the slight attention I used to bestow upon Christina Braun. Our bass singer did not always come with us to Miss Griffin's, and even when he did he was not much of a squire of dames or demoiselles. On entering the little drawing-room—first-floor front, over a bonnet-shop—he usually laid his hat somewhere on the ground, sat on the edge of a chair, swallowed his tea, bending far over the table for the purpose, and generally said nothing more than "Yes, miss," or "No, miss," in answer to any question addressed to him. He was a fine-looking young fellow, tall, robust, manly; and, although scarcely

older than myself, he had his face already fringed
with a luxuriant, soft, black beard, the possession
of which I secretly envied him. Silent as he
was in general, I could notice that when he got
side by side with Christina Braun he could talk
well enough to her; and almost always when he
came to Miss Griffin's, I observed that he took
charge of Christina to see her to her home on
our early breaking up. I think I was somewhat
amused at the time by observing this fact and
founding conjectures on it. The polite reader
need hardly be told that a much loftier position
in society is asserted by a lawyer's clerk than
could possibly be claimed even by the most pre-
sumptuous carpenter; and I therefore felt myself
warranted in taking quite a lordly and patronising
interest in the love-making of my humble acquaintance; for I felt convinced that our stout
basso was in love, and I envied him that privilege.
Yes, more even than his beard did I envy him his
state of mind and heart. At this season of my
life I had begun to long to fall in love. I envied
every young man whom I saw on Sunday evening
with some girl hanging on his arm or walking
with downcast eyes by his side. I trolled out to

myself of nights the words of "Sally in our Alley;" and I envied the hero of the ballad, for all his harsh master and his jeering neighbours. If some woman would only love me, walk thus of Sundays with me, lean on my arm, blush when I spoke! Nay, if some woman would even reject my love, blight my young hopes, crush me in the bud, reduce me to despair! At the stage of mental and moral development I had then reached, despair and ruin seemed on the whole a finer and more enviable destiny than success and joy. To live in love would be happy; but to die for love would be the lordliest fate.

My life seemed safe enough so far as love's despair could threaten it. I had no one to love. I could not, no I could not, love Miss Griffin, strove I never so wildly. I feel well assured she would have accepted gladly the poorest tribute of homage, even if it lasted but a few short weeks, to cheat her into the belief that she had not quite passed out of date, and could yet move at least one heart. All our literature and our moral lessons now ring the changes upon the nobleness of self-sacrifice. What finer self-sacrifice could any-one make than to persuade a kind and true-hearted old maid of a certain age that he had really fallen in love with her, and brighten her life by giving up his own to sustain the beatifying delusion? A more pious fraud could not be accomplished than to practise such a generous piece of cheating on such a woman as poor, elderly, warm-hearted, loving, unloved Miss Griffin. I commend the idea to some novelist. Why not make a story out of it? But I own that, even had the idea occurred to me at the right time, I should not have dreamed of putting it into practice; and even if I had dreamed of it, I should never have done it.

There was none of Miss Griffin's pupils who could have served as an object for my adoration. They were all in trousers and short frocks; and at that time of my life girls in trousers were my abhorrence.

When haply my thoughts sometimes turned to Christina Braun, she seemed too calm and silent, and too fond of music. In those days I did not much care for any singing but my own. There are only too many people who, if they would but confess it, are in just the same state of mind —people who have, of course, none of the true

artist's love of music, as, honestly, I never had.
People like us in that way often delight in our
own singing, if we can sing, not out of mere self-
conceit and egotism, but because to us that music
which our own voices give out is the fullest expression, the strongest invocation, of feeling and
association. Many tenors of the richest tone,
and sopranos thrilling up to the ceiling, have I
heard without feeling one throb of the emotion
which used to swell within me long ago as I sang
old church-hymns or new sentimental ballads of
love, longing, and despair for my own delight,
and quite alone. But it was easy enough even
for me then to see that Christina Braun loved
music for its own sake, and, like most persons
who do thus appreciate and love it, she seemed,
to ordinary observers, to care about little else.

Apart from all this, however, I had arranged
in my own mind that Christina Braun and the
carpenter's son were what we used to call "sweet-
hearts."

After some time I began to observe that Christina ceased to make one in our mild gatherings in
Miss Griffin's drawing-room. Indeed the latter
lady and I sometimes had tea *tête-à-tête*—or nearly

so, her mother only flitting flightily in and out—
and it was dull entertainment for both parties.
I would gladly have evaded all such *soirées*, but
that I was ashamed or unwilling to desert poor
Miss Griffin, and perhaps did not always know
what to do with myself or where else to go. The
time for sitting alone in contented gloom, and
smoking a pipe long evenings through, had not
nearly come as yet.

Sometimes a fearful thought crossed my mind.
Could it be possible that Christina imagined Miss
Griffin and I were lovers, and liked to be left
alone? I tried to shut out this alarming idea.
I vowed not to go any more to a *tête-à-tête* tea;
I even attempted awkwardly to pay a mild attention to Christina herself, in the hope of thus re-
pelling suspicion. I invited her to come with me
to a concert somewhere—we had not the rules of
Belgravia or even Bloomsbury to govern our social
relationships there—but Christina refused in so
decided a tone as to make my doubts a dead
certainty. I began to feel convinced that I had
guessed but too well. Christina must suppose
me deeply in love with Miss Griffin—perhaps solemnly engaged to her—to Miss Griffin, whose

age was so undeniable, and who carried the stigma of old maid branded on her very skirts and ankles!

One evening we three—we three!—walked home together, as usual, but were unusually dull and silent. Christina declined entering when we arrived at Miss Griffin's door—this time indeed the invitation being very faintly pressed. I was plucking up heart of grace to make my excuses too, when Miss Griffin cut me short by a look of portentous mystery, and the words, "You really must come in, Mr. Banks; I want to speak to you"—words which, however, were not spoken until just after Christina had nodded her head to us and gone on her way.

I followed Miss Griffin upstairs in perhaps something like an agitated condition of mind. I did not quite know whether under certain circumstances strong-minded ladies not young did not think it allowable to interrogate young men touching the nature of their intentions.

Miss Griffin was anything but a strong-minded woman, and just now did not seem to have been thinking about me at all. She burst out with her communication all at once.

"O Mr. Banks, I must send Christina Braun"

(pronounced, as I have said before, "Brawn")
"out of the choir. She must not sing with us
any more."

Did I feel relieved to hear that the question
was of Christina's rejection, and not of my ac-
ceptance? Perhaps so. But I certainly felt
much surprised.

" What on earth has she been doing?"

" I am so sorry to hear it; indeed, it's quite
put me out; you can't think how much."

" Yes; but what is it?"

" I am afraid she is not a good girl. She
sings every night at a singing-house!"

" At a singing-house?"

" Yes; a common low singing-house, Mr.
Banks—and I don't see what there is to laugh at
—a horrid place where soldiers and sailors and I
don't know what—all sorts of low people, in fact
—go in and drink and listen to her. It's been all
found out; and Mr. Thirlwall (the clergyman)
says he can't have a girl in the choir who sings
for soldiers and sailors in a common drinking-
house. I don't know what to do about it; and
I declare it has put me in such a way, you can't
think. Perhaps she is not so bad; and then it's

all very well for Mr. Thirlwall to talk, but, my goodness, who is to fill her place, with such a voice as she has, and such an ear for music? But I can't keep her unless she promises never to go there any more."

"Then you have not spoken to her yet about it?"

"No, not yet. I thought I would ask you something about it first. I thought perhaps you could advise me; you, who are a man of business and know something about the world."

"Well, I am sure I don't see much harm in the whole affair, and I think Mr. Thirlwall is a venerable goose. Miss Braun seems a very quiet, respectable sort of girl" (I thought of the carpenter's love-suit, and felt quite a lordly spirit of patronising pity); "and then what can she do if she's very poor and has no other way of living? The reverend man does not expect her to live on fifteen pounds a-year, paid in rather irregular instalments?"

"Yes, that is all quite true; and indeed it is just what I said myself to Mr. Thirlwall—only of course I put it more politely—and *he* says it is true too; for he's a just man, Mr. Banks, though

you always seem inclined to laugh at him. But
what can he do? He has been preaching from
the pulpit time after time against those very sing-
ing-houses, and how can he have people looking
up from their seats in the church, and perhaps
some of them recognising a singer from such a
place among the faces in our choir? You know
yourself that would never do."

It occurred to me at the moment that perhaps
the worshipper who visited the wicked singing-
house, and was thereby enabled to recognise one
of its performers, would have scarcely a clear right
to object to the chorister who sang there. But
I saw no use in urging this point to a logical conclusion, and merely suggested that perhaps the
place was not so dreadfully bad after all.

"That is what I was just thinking of. I
should really like to know something of it. It
would never do to give up the poor girl without
knowing whether there is any harm in what she
is doing. I actually thought of going there myself; I did really."

"O, you can't go, that is quite out of the
question; but if you like I'll go, and bring you a
faithful report."

"That is what I should like of all things. I can depend upon your judgment. And at all events one ought to know something about the right and wrong of the affair. I believe in law, Mr. Banks, a person is innocent until you can prove her guilty."

"That is considered one of the great principles of British law, Miss Griffin."

"Yes; and I think it's very proper too; and I only wish people would do the same in everything else as well as law."

It was settled, then, that I was to visit and report on the obnoxious singing-place. I had heard of it once or twice before; and of sundry of its predecessors which had all in succession withered and disappeared. Up to this time I had never been out of my native town, and of course had never been in a singing-saloon. Our town was an unspeakably dull spot. At this time it was not even visited by a railway, and it depended for its sole excitement upon the changing of a regiment in the barracks or the occasional visit of a war-frigate to the harbour. Owing to the social and topographical peculiarities I have already mentioned which divided us, like all Gaul in Cæ-

sar's day, into three parts, any sort of amusement
which might be devised for the gratification of
the floating population in the lower plateau, was
not likely to excite either interest or alarm in the
higher regions. Our middle class were little given
to revelry. Every window in their quarter was
duly shuttered and barred by eleven o'clock, and
their warmest stimulant was a controversial sermon. But of late there had unquestionably been
some stir created by the successful establishment,
after many failures, of a famous singing-saloon,
modelled after the fashion of metropolitan dissi-
pation. Not a noisy, harmless "free-and-easy,"
where Snug the joiner and Quince the carpenter
might smoke their pipes and be knocked down in
turn for their favourite and special song; where
Bottom the weaver might deliver his choicest sentiment, and Starveling the tailor might have the
formal permission of his wife to remain half-an-
hour later on the Saturday night. This was not
the sort of thing that now invaded us. It was a
place where professional singers—women too, look
you, nearly as bad as dancers, not to say actresses
—came and sat on a platform, and sang for money.
This was then a dreadful innovation. The sing-

ing-saloon itself is now well-nigh obsolete. The rising generation hardly knows what it was like. The music-hall with its plate-glass, its paintings, its private boxes, its concerted music and its champagne, has banished it; and the audacious novelty of my young days is a forgotten, fogeyish old institution now. But this particular place of which I speak was really creating something like a stir among our quiet and respectable burgesses just then. It was established immediately inside the frontier line of our Alsatia; and it is certain that some of our fathers of families had been to visit it, and had talked with quite a dangerous slyness of its attractions, and had made up parties with some of their friends to go and see it again. All this created naturally a considerable fluttering of angry petticoats in domestic circles, and brought severe and direct condemnation from offended pulpits. And so I had heard of the place in question, and had even been making up my mind to visit it before chance sent me there as the special commissioner of Miss Griffin.

The following night I went alone, and had no difficulty in finding the place. Indeed, when you began to descend from the old square, which was the last stronghold of respectability and middle class, down a steep street with steps breaking its precipitate fall, a street that was the main artery of the lower town, you came almost at once upon the obnoxious saloon. It was in a large public-house, occupying a corner where a cross-street ran off, and showing, like Janus, a double front. The place looked cheery enough from the outside. The night was chill and wet; and the bright crimson curtains draping the windows of the upper room where the musical performances were going on, tempted one with visions of ineffable comfort and warmth out of the wintry plash and drizzle of the sodden streets. I went upstairs. There was no payment at the doors, the musical entertainment being supported in the recognised style by indirect taxation levied upon the "orders." I entered the Circean bower. It was but a small and poor imitation of a Strand or Covent Garden Cave of Harmony, but as it had looking-glasses, crimson curtains, velvet cushions, a platform with footlights, and an orchestra, it seemed splendid enough in my confused provincial eyes. I gave an order for something in a rather ineffectual attempt at a careless tone, and dropped into the

first available seat. There was rather a numerous
audience, including, however, only one or two
sailors and no soldiers. Most of the company
seemed to me to be smart young artisans, mingled
with elderly tradesmen of the unpretentious class;
and there were a few young assistants from shops
who looked quite swellish in their well-made
clothes and gloves. No ladies were there; Miss
Griffin would have presented herself in vain.
Most of the company were smoking, by which I
was innocently surprised to find that the singers
were not in the least disconcerted. Of the "audience," a very few were actually listening to the
music; the greater number were chatting unconcernedly round their little tables; one or two
were asleep. I had, however, listened with the
gravest appearance of interest to a sentimental
and a comic song before I came to myself sufficiently to observe even this much of the aspect
of the place.

When I said there were no women present, I
meant, of course, among the audience. For when
I began to look collectedly around me, I saw that
there were girls on the platform, and that among
them was Christina Braun. She was dressed in

white—poor white muslin only; but she seemed
to my eyes to be wearing a magnificent costume.
Her arms and shoulders were bare, and were both
white and plump, and her fleece of light hair fell
around her. She presently came on to sing, and
she seemed to be a favourite, for she was welcomed by a burst of applause, and most of the
company stopped their talk, while some demanded
silence by tapping their pipe-bowls on the table.
Christina sang in clear and strong tones some
ballad—not at all a Circean strain, but some good
moral-purpose song about universal brotherhood
and being kind to our neighbour. She sang it
with sweetness and force, but with hardly any
indication of feeling, certainly with no gleam of
emotion perceptible in her eyes. Being, however,
vehemently encored, she chose, as seemed to be
expected, a totally different kind of song. It was
what we used to call a "nigger melody"—a sort
of novelty then, with a refrain about courting down
in Tennessee, or Alabama, or some other such
place.

I scarcely knew what it was all about; but I
soon knew that I had never heard such spirit,
such archness, such wild wayward humour, such

occasional ebullitions of tender thrilling emotion conveyed in song before. No, never! Night after night had I heard this girl sing her devotional hymns in the clearest tones, vacant of any emotion whatever; but now, as she sang some trumpery little serio-comic love-song, her dark-gray eyes gleamed and filled with light; under her shadowy long lashes the eyes sometimes looked so dark and deep as to seem in startling contrast with her bright fair hair; her voice swelled, soared, sank, shaded itself away into an infinite variety of expression; she gave life and speech to the very rattle of her banjo; she made the ballad utter a thousand emotions which were no more in the words she sang than in the instrument she struck, or the smoky, beery crowd, whose glasses jingled with their noisy and honest acclamations. What a soul of feeling, what a capacity—deep, boundless, daring—a capacity for love and triumph, and passion and sorrow—spoke in the tones of that voice and the flash of that eye!

For me, I felt partly as I used to feel when sitting alone and singing, only with how much of a difference! With what a change from dreamy, vague, and fluctuating emotions, idly rolling in like the waves on the windless shore, and the warm, tumultuous, passionate rush of the new tide of love and youth and manhood breaking in upon my life at last! I began life, I began love, with the hearing of that song! I daresay it was poor, coarse, untutored singing; untrained, and even in some sense uncouth, it must have been; commonplace it certainly was not. I know that I heard the singer unnumbered times in the prime of her years and her triumph; and I do not believe I ever recognised her genius more clearly than when I heard her sing that poor little ballad in the public-house of the old sea-port. My rapture must upon that occasion find some outlet, and I therefore made instant acquaintance with a dull and elderly man near me: he seemed to me, I don't know why, to look like a saddler.

"Splendid!" I exclaimed, addressing him.

"Yes, pretty tidy," rejoined the dull man; and he looked round for the waiter and knocked his empty glass against the table—a signal for a refilling.

"I know her," I added confidentially.

" Know who ?" asked the dull man.

" Her—the singer."

" Ah !" He did not seem to care whether I knew her or not.

" She's a foreigner," I added, especially proud of knowing a foreigner.

"Ah, I never liked the French—I don't believe in 'em. By what I can make out, they ain't good for much."

" But she's not French—she's German."

" Don't like Germans, they're a dirty set. They eat candles, I'm told."

This irrelevant and detestable observation so utterly disgusted me, that I withdrew at once from the conversation.

I should much have liked to wait for the close of the entertainment and to speak to Christina; but I feared she might suppose I had come as a spy or tell-tale, so I slunk very much indeed as if I were a spy or tell-tale from my seat, which was near the door, and went downstairs. I did not gain much by my caution and my flight, for, descending rapidly, I ran against someone coming as rapidly up, and I recognised my friend the basso, the bearded young carpenter. We saluted

each other, but he did not seem particularly glad
to see me, and he ran past without staying to
speak a word. I wished I had not met him, for
I feared that in the too-probable event of poor
Christina's dismissal, he might regard me and
report me as a spy, and I had an instinctive
knowledge that he had come to see her home;
and I envied him—nay, already I almost hated
him.

Drizzling and dismal as the black skies were,
sloppy and slushy as the streets were, I did not
hurry home. On the contrary, I turned deliberately away from home, and straggled, like the
town, downhill to the water. From the door I
had just quitted I could hear the creaking of the
spars of ships that tossed and dragged at their
anchors, the whistling of the sullen wind through
their cordage, the heavy surge of the waves along
their sides. A few strides down an oozy lane,
and I could see the lights at mastheads, and even
discern through the mist and darkness the white
tops of the rushing waves. I made my way,
stumbling among upturned boats and anchors
and chains, down to the very edge of the water.
The town was not well-lighted anywhere : towards

the harbour its darkness grew Cimmerian. The
inhabitants had all that mysterious objection to
seeing their seaward way at night which used to
be so common a characteristic of people living in
seaport towns in the years when French treaties
were not. Indeed, many of our people would
have abolished moonlight if they could, although
these very same persons were strangely given to
lurking about the shore and staring seaward at
extraordinary hours of the night. This night,
however, no stealthy figure peered from the
strand: I had it all to myself, and I exulted in
being alone.

Born as I was within sound of the waves, it
has always seemed to me that in any hour of deep
emotion I ought to rush to the seaside, and make
the noisy water my confidant. This night I felt
that I must find the shore, and relieve my new-
born passion by mingling its utterances with the
roar of the waters. Alone on that strand what
strange fooleries I enacted! I stamped up and
down the shore, I sang wild snatches of Christina's song, I shouted mad fragments of inco-
herent melody and semi - articulate words of
passion and love. I was mad, and I was happy;

this at last was living. All the delight that an explorer may find when he first breaks into a new sea—that a Bedouin may feel when he first mounts an untamed horse—I felt, now that I knew myself to be tossing at last on the waves of passionate love.

Lucky for me that I was alone, and that the night was so dark. Anyone seeing my gestures, hearing my cries, must have taken me for a lunatic. I waited on the strand until my emotions had worked off their first vehemence; perhaps I waited too until I thought the entertainment at the singing-saloon must be nearly over. Then I went back to the street whence I had come, and watched the people coming out. After the last of the audience had melted away, came out a cluster of the performers; among them I could clearly enough distinguish the figure of Christina —I had keen eyes for her form now—and my friend the basso was escorting her home. A strange, fierce pang shot through me. I had learned to feel two new passions in a few short hours—love and jealousy.

CHAPTER III.

I DID not go near Miss Griffin next day. I post-poned making any report of my previous night's visitation. What report could I make but that I had been present at a very dull and harmless entertainment? unless I chose to add the truth —that I had come away madly in love with the eyes and the voice of a girl whom I had been in the habit of seeing three or four times a week for months and months, and about whom I never before cared a straw. Mine was certainly not love at first sight, but it had all the suddenness and unreasoning fierceness of that romantic form of the passion. I have not read in books much about such a love as mine, which neither flamed out at the first glimpse of the object, nor grew up with the gradual development of intimacy and appreciation. I was as one who walks in the sun of some tropical climate uninjured and un-

heeding for days, and whom suddenly, in some
unexpecting moment, a flash, sharp as the cleave
of a sabre, strikes and cuts down. Yes, my love
was like a sunstroke. I do not know how to
describe it better.

Of course I went again to the music-house;
I went the next night. The company was of the
same general character; the singers were the
same. The moment I entered I saw that Christina's eyes turned on me, and I blushed like a
great girl. Some male singer came on with his
dreary comic song, and she disappeared from the
platform. Had she gone for the night? What
a cruel disappointment! I stared disconsolate
and confounded into my beer-glass, and was
positively pitying myself for my privation, when
one of the waiters, who were perpetually buzzing
about the tables to remind any laggard guests
of the necessity of renewing their orders, came
up to me, and leaning over my shoulder, said,

" Lady wants to speak to you, sir."

I started.

" Lady !—what lady ?"

" Profesh'nal lady, sir. Behind the platform,
sir. This way, please."

I followed him. I was crimson all over, and did not venture to look up, fearing that the eyes of a whole curious company must be fixed on me. As a matter of fact, I don't suppose anybody in the room took the slightest notice. I was trembling with anxiety, hope, fear, surprise, excitement of the most complicated kind. The waiter drew aside a curtain for me, and I entered a small sanded room, or rather a mere space, behind the platform; and I saw Christina there alone.

She had her head turned away when I came in: at the sound of my entrance she looked quickly round, and there was an angry light in her deep-gray eyes.

Her first words utterly abashed me.

"Why do you come here?" she said, in a voice purposely kept low, and with the foreign accent more strongly perceptible than usual, owing to the kind of excitement under which she spoke. "Why do you come here to watch me and tell bad of me? Have I ever done you any harm?"

"O Christina,—Miss Braun, I mean,—how can you say such a thing?" and I broke down in mere stammering.

"Have you not come here to watch me—to spy on me?"

"No. I have not, indeed."

"It's a lie!" she exclaimed, so loudly that I involuntarily glanced in the direction of the audience, fearing the words must have been heard. "It's an untruth. I know you were sent here."

"I was not sent here. Miss Griffin asked me to come here; and—"

"And you came!"

She made a triumphant gesture expressive of conviction and scorn. I certainly felt not unlike a detected spy; and I looked, no doubt, very foolish.

"Yes, I came; but I did not come to—to find out anything bad, or to do you harm. I came to do you good; and Miss Griffin only wanted to do you good."

"Thank you both." She laid a malicious emphasis on the word 'both.' "I am much obliged to you both. Heartfelt thanks to you both. But I don't want anyone to try to do me good."

"I wished to be your friend."

"I have not many friends—I am poor and

miserable; and I have an old man to support whom I love and whom I would die for; and you come and find out that I am trying to make a living, and without wrong to anyone, or myself, or God, and you tell of me at the church. Go away; it is not like a man. It is not like an Englishman."

"But I swear to you, Miss Braun, that you are wrong and unjust. You don't know me, or you never would speak as you have done. I am utterly incapable of the wretched meanness you think me guilty of. I wish I could say all I feel, but I can't—I can't; and I daresay I look to you like a convicted spy, or an idiot, or something equally abominable."

" You came last night to see if I was here?"

" I did."

" So! You saw that I was here?"

" I did."

" Then was that not enough? Why did you come again to-night?"

" I came to hear you sing! Heaven knows I came for that and nothing else. It—it delights me. I could not stay away. I will come again and again, unless you bid me not. But do not

bid me not to come, for I would rather be dead
than not hear you sing."

"Hush," she said in a low and gentle tone,
"they outside may hear us." As I found courage
to look up, I saw that her lips were trembling and
that her cheeks were crimsoned. Had my burst
of sudden eloquence not been interrupted, it would
infallibly have ended with a fervent declaration of
love then and there. She imposed silence on me
by a gesture which had, I thought, as much en-
treaty as command in it, and then said, " I must
go; it is my time to sing. But I believe you;
and I was wrong and angry. You don't know
what it is to be a poor girl, trying to live honestly,
and watched and suspected. I beg you for pardon. Good-night."

She disappeared; and I heard her voice in a
moment thrilling from the platform. I, too, came
in front again, and found my way back to the seat
I had left.

I would have sat the whole entertainment out,
but that I hated the idea of meeting the young
carpenter and seeing him give his arm to Christina. I waited and waited, every moment dread-
ing to see him make his appearance. Often as I

turned towards the platform, her eyes never met mine. At last I made up my mind and left the room. Luck was against me; at the door below I met my rival. This time he did not pass me with a salute. He looked fiercely at me, and his lips quivered with excitement.

"What d'ye come here for?" he asked.

"What's that to you?" was my schoolboyish reply. I was not in years much beyond the schoolboy age.

"It's this to me—look here, it's this: you come here to watch that girl, and spy upon her, and fetch and carry stories about her, to get her dismissed from the choir; I daresay that's why you come here."

"You are a liar!" was my fierce reply—"an impertinent liar!"

He turned pale; but not at all with fear.

"Do you mean to say," he asked, "that you've not been sent here as a spy on her?"

"I mean to say nothing to you, or any fellow like you, except just what I have said."

"Yes, you can talk in that way *here*," he said significantly; "but would you say so anywhere else?"

"Anywhere you like ; and the sooner the better." My pent-up feelings sought any manner of outburst as a relief.

"Come this way, then."

My rival led the way, down the oozy plashy lane I have already described, to the strand. It was nearly as dark as the night before : it was quite as lonely. The few twinkling lights at the far mastheads of anchored vessels alone broke the gloom. Unless we stood pretty close together we could hardly see each other, and my foe strode on so impatiently that I sometimes lost sight of him altogether for a moment, and I was once or twice almost under the necessity of having to raise an undignified halloo. How he managed to get on without stumbling I cannot imagine ; every other moment my feet were tripping over huge stones, or coils of chain, and once I literally fell forward right over an upturned boat. I began to think the whole proceeding rather an absurd one ; but I had been grievously insulted, and although now a minion of the law, professionally bound, one would think, to abstain from deeds of vio-lence, yet it must be remembered that I was the son of a boat-builder who had been a sailor in his day, and that not many months ago I was a schoolboy. Yet I much wished the duel to come off quickly, and while my blood was up; for I felt the ridiculous features of the business becoming every moment more impressive, and I began to think that an attorney's clerk boxing with a carpenter — a poetic and musical young lover fighting a vulgar rival with fists — would be outrageously absurd, unpicturesque, and un-heroic.

At last my pertinacious and thrice-accursed tormentor came to a pause on a clear spot, or what seemed clear.

"Now then," he said, "there's nobody here. What have you got to say? Are you not a spy and a sneak?"

This was too much; and as I had given my answer in words before, I thought a repetition of it would be mere tautology. I was glad, too, to bring my scruples and hesitations to a violent end. I simply hit out, and caught my antago-nist fairly on the left eyebrow.

Then began the fight. It was hearty, vigor-ous, and funny. I don't know whether many of my readers have fought a battle on the seashore

at an advanced hour of a dark winter night. The
sensations it produces are decidedly odd, tanta-
lising and bewildering; but it has its peculiar
enjoyment too. At least, this battle of mine
seemed a positively delightful relief from my previous frame of mind. I very soon found that my
antagonist was far stronger than I. He had indeed arms of iron; and he took his punishment
with unruffled countenance. The punishment
was pretty hard, for he had no gleam whatever
of scientific knowledge, and exposed himself constantly to a smart blow on the face. But he
seemed to care no more for the blows than if
they had been the pepperings of a hail-shower,
although, dark as it was, I could see that his
face was bleeding in many places. His mode of
fighting was an odd and self-acquired process
altogether. He never hit straight out, but level-
led huge, tremendous, swinging blows at the side
of the head, literally leaping off his feet at each
stroke, so as to lend it a more furious momentum.
I was inclined to laugh at first, but I soon found
it was no laughing matter, for the first touch I
got of one of these odd blows—and I only got a
touch, for I sprang aside in time—nearly knocked

all my senses clear away. If he had been prompt
to follow up his victory, the combat was over
there and then! As it was, I felt pretty sure
that should I be unlucky enough to come in for
the full force and swing of one of those swash-
ing blows, it would be enough for me; and I
tried with desperate energy all such resources of
science and strength as I had to bring the fight
to a conclusion. He bore my hammering as
coolly as if he were of iron; and alas! I think
he acquired at last a sort of rude notion of strata-
gem wholly his own. He threw himself quite
open in the most tempting fashion to one of my
straightforward blows, took it without even shaking his head, and while I was in the very act of
giving it, suddenly leaped upright, swung his
huge flail of an arm, and crash across the side
of my head came all the full fury of his blow.
Meteors in a moment danced and sparkled all
around me; stars, comets, flashes of lightning
blazed upon my eyes; thunders indescribable
rattled round my ears and brain; the earth heaved
beneath me; the dark sky came crashing down
upon me. I seemed as if I were cast loose from
all gravitating principle and whirling through

space, now head up, now heels up—and at last
I came with a cruel bang down to earth again
—and then I felt for half a second a soft, sweet,
melting sensation of languid rest, like that pro-
duced to a bruised man by the bleeding of a vein,
and I just heard something like a shriek, and
then I was asleep.

The plain practical English of all my sensations was that I had been fairly knocked off
my feet by a stunning blow, had fallen with my
head crashing against a stone, and had then and
there fainted.

When I opened my eyes I saw at first nothing
but the stars. I remained feebly contemplating
them a moment, as if that were all I had to
do in existence. Then I saw some dark object
interpose itself between me and the constellation
of Orion, and I recognised the face of my con-
queror, and I think I endeavoured to frown de-
fiance; but the face was in a moment withdrawn.
Then I somehow became conscious that a soft
hand was passing along my forehead, that a hand-
kerchief, or something of the kind, was pressed
gently but firmly on the place where the stone
had cut me; and at last I came to understand

that I was lying on the beach with my head in a woman's lap.

Unconsciously I spoke half aloud the word "Christina!"

"O, thank God!" said Christina's own voice, "he's alive."

"Yes, thank God!" muttered the deep voice of the poor basso; "I didn't mean to do it, Christina—I didn't indeed. I wish he had done it to me."

"For shame!" replied Christina, still in a sort of whisper. "Shame to you—so strong and huge—to fight with him."

I began now to see things a little clearer; and I scrambled to my feet, still somewhat staggery, perhaps, but quite able to speak up for myself.

"It's no fault of his," I said; "and I'm quite well able to fight him. Look at his face, Miss Braun, and see if he hasn't got the worst of it. And it was all my fault, too."

Christina rose to her feet. "Now, shake hands," she said, "and don't be fools any more."

My antagonist advanced sheepishly and held

out the brawny fist which had proved such a
rough playfellow.

"I—I hope you'll forgive me," he said, with
one glance at me and another at Christina. "I
was quite wrong altogether; and I know it now,
and I'm sorry. I'm sure I don't bear any malice,
if you don't; and—and—how do you feel now?"

I assured him, in all sincerity, that I bore
no malice whatever; and I likewise affirmed, perhaps not quite so sincerely, that I felt perfectly
well — never better in my life. Indeed, I was
recovering fast. I had only had a stunning blow
and a cut head. At twenty years one soon gets
over such trifles as these.

I then learned that when Christina was leaving the singing-room she inquired for her regular
escort, and was told that he had gone down towards the strand with me. Something led her
to suspect that we had quarrelled, and she followed us, but arrived only in time to witness the
ignominious fall and utter defeat of one combat-
ant. I ought to have been delighted at my defeat, for it brought such tender interest and
anxiety about me; but I was not delighted. The
one thing present to my mind all through was

that I had been "licked," and that *she* saw it.
"Earl Percy sees my fall," is the reflection that
lends most bitterness to the fate of the old hero
in the ballad. What is the humiliation of a chief
before any foe compared with that of a youth
who is beaten under the very eyes of the girl
he loves? The pity and kindness of Christina
were bitter to me.

On the other hand, my rival's victory did not
seem to have crowned him with joy. He had a
crestfallen, humbled, spaniel-like demeanour. We
both walked home with Christina, who insisted
on giving me her arm instead of taking mine,
on the ground that I must be far too weak not
to need support.

When we reached her door I heard my con-
queror say to her in a low tone,

"You are not angry with me any more?"

"No," was the answer, given, I am bound to
say, in anything but a forgiving tone. "Why
should I be angry? Good-night!"

"Ah, but you are angry. Don't, Christina!"

"Good-night."

He was going away, depressed and silent,
when she called him back and held out her hand.

"No, Edward, I am not angry. I was, but I am not any more."

"And may I come for you to-morrow night?"

"If you like!"

"If I like!"

He turned away rejoicing.

She held out her hand to me without saying a word. But her eyes met mine: and somehow I went away rejoicing too.

Next day I called upon Miss Griffin. I hardly knew what to say to the good spinster, and was much in hope, as I passed up through the bonnet-shop, that the organist might be not at home. She was in. I went upstairs and knocked at the little drawing - room door. Just then I heard voices inside, and I would have retreated; but it was too late. Miss Griffin's shrill tones were heard:

"Is that Mr. Banks?"

"Yes, Miss Griffin."

"Come in, Mr. Banks, please."

I entered. Miss Griffin was standing up near her piano, on which she rested one hand, the fingers of which were excitedly playing an imaginary and rapid tune on the walnut. Christina

Braun stood in the middle of the room, and
looked flushed and angry. My face flushed more
deeply than hers at the mere sight of her. Miss
Griffin's mamma was playing with a parrot in a
corner. Seeing that Christina and Miss Griffin
had evidently been engaged in exciting colloquy,
I made for the mamma, and would have at once
pretended to bury myself in conversation with
her, but she waved me off with the back of her
hand and with a warning gesture directed towards the two principal personages in the room,
as one who should say, " Forbear, young man ;
something highly important is going forward.
Disturb it not by idle words." So I stood trans-
fixed and said nothing, and no one said a word
to me.

"There's no use in talking, Christina Braun,"
Miss Griffin went on ; " I can't have you singing
any longer in my choir unless you give up that
horrid, odious, abominable place. Mr. Thirlwall
won't have it ; he would not allow me to have anyone who sings there."

"What harm is that place ?" Christina asked
in a tone half-pleading, half-angry ; " I would not
go there if I could help it. I go there, believe it,

not for my pleasure. I go there because I must live, and my father must live. You have not a father, Miss Griffin."

Mamma pursed her mouth, raised her eye-brows, lifted her hands, and silently appealed, first to me and then to the parrot, against the boldness of this remark. It seemed positively to insinuate a comparison between Christina's father and the late Mr. Griffin.

"And," added Christina, "they pay me more money than the church can give."

"O Christina!"

"I speak to no one there."

"But you must know it is not a proper place for a girl."

"I do not know that it is not a proper place. Did we not often sing songs,—yes, well, and also play waltzes, in the choir when there were not people praying below?"

"Christina, it isn't the singing of the songs, as you know very well; it's the people—the kind of people who go there."

"I do not speak to the people, they do not speak to me, except they who sing as myself."

"Really, Miss Griffin," said I, striking in,

"there is no harm whatever in the place, and I think it's quite absurd and ridiculous of Mr. Thirlwall to go on in such a way. He's a regular old idiot, I think, and an ancient humbug too."

"Thank you, Mr. Banks; I am much obliged to you for your kind and respectful way of speaking of our clergyman, and the considerate manner in which you assist me in keeping up the discipline of the choir. For you, Christina, you do not know what may become of you."

"Nothing will become of me, God helping,— nothing of harm. And I may as well begin, Miss Griffin. Once I shall go upon the theatre and sing there—"

At this point Miss Griffin seemed to think the discussion had gone quite far enough. She ceased to beat her silent tune upon the piano; but she came round to the front of the instrument, deliberately took off the music-book which stood on the little frame, shut the book up, put down the frame, and then closed the piano with a solemn bang. There was no obvious occasion for this performance. I interpreted it to be a sort of formal and ceremonial act of excommunication.

It seemed, however, to have relieved Miss

Griffin's mind of some of its anger. She turned to Christina now with an expression of face rather grieved than severe. The excommunication once fairly done, she seemed stricken with pity for the outcast.

"Well, Christina," she said, "if I am to understand that you will not give up that place—"

"Will not give it up? I cannot give it up."

"Then I am very, very sorry; and I would keep you if I could—indeed I would, although perhaps you don't think it now; but I must not do it, for you see, Christina, if you have a father to support, I have a mother, and I can't battle against what people say; and so we must part. I hope you will do well, Christina, wherever you go; only I do hope you will never be tempted to sing in any of those Romanist places, whatever they may offer you; and remember to be a good girl, and never to give up your church."

"The church," said Christina, with a flash of something like scorn crossing her face, "has given me up, I think. But I blame you not at all, Miss Griffin; you were very kind to me always — always."

Poor Miss Griffin was quite dissolved in tears.

The very kindliest of mortals, she was in anguish at the part she had to play in the transaction, and still more, I fully believe, at the thought of the awful ruin of all heavenly prospects which she clearly saw impending over one who refused to follow the behests of her clergyman, and who sang nigger-melodies for sailors.

Christina bade Miss Griffin good-bye; and both were in tears. Then the outcast walked towards Miss Griffin's mamma and held out her hand. But the mamma's dignity was hurt at the disobedience and disrespect, and she drew back, executed the most formal of bows, and said, "Adieu, mademoiselle."

Then came my turn. Christina held out her hand to me, and her eyes met mine. I took her hand and pressed it to my lips. A slight shriek from mamma testified to her sense of my scandalous conduct. Miss Griffin was absorbed in tears and did not see it.

Christina left the room, and I hurried after her.

"Mr. Banks," I heard Miss Griffin call out, "please don't go yet. I want to speak to you particularly—about the choir."

"In five minutes, two minutes, Miss Griffin,"

was my retreating answer; and I relieved myself by adding, in a lower tone, "the choir may go to the devil."

I overtook Christina at the door.

She abandoned the choir, then and there, never reappearing within its precincts.

And I went that night, and many nights successively, to the condemned and fatal singing-saloon.

In little more than a week a considerable change was brought about in the relations of the personages of this story. There was first a sort of break-down in the arrangements of the choir, and one Sunday the audience had to be content with merely an instrumental performance. Soon a new bass, a new tenor, and a new soprano gladdened the pious ears and hearts of the congregation. For immediately on Christina's abandoning the choir Ned Lambert did what I had felt sure he would do—he gave up his post and sang bass for that congregation no more. I had made up my mind never to go near the place again, once Christina abandoned it; and I was only sorry the sacrifice was not a far greater one (really it was not quite insignificant), that I might have

had the proud consciousness of voluntary martyr-
dom.

The affair created quite a little stir in our
microcosm. It was talked of for fully three weeks
—at least, three Sundays. I attended church the
first Sunday, as unprofessional worshipper, in the
hope that Mr. Thirlwall might make some allusion
to us in his sermon. But he did not, and I was
disappointed. Many eyes were turned on me,
however, and people coming out of church and
passing me whispered and shrugged their shoulders; and I felt rather proud. The general conclusion of the congregation was that we three—
Christina Braun, Edward Lambert, and myself—
were simply going to the devil.

CHAPTER IV.

Mr. Braun and his daughter still occupied the house in which the former had endeavoured in vain to win the childhood of our town to philosophy and science by the royal road of amusement. Our childhood absolutely refused even toys, if any manner of instruction and moral purpose were to come with them; and therefore, while Mr. Braun still technically occupied the house, his actual occupancy was confined to three small rooms on the second-floor. He had been driven back in this way from stage to stage, his domain growing gradually smaller and smaller, like the Pope's, until even the little Leonine City now left him seemed itself only the final halting-place before absolute surrender of all temporal endowment. The shop was let to a watchmaker; the first-floor was occupied by a hair-dresser; and as one of the plates on the street-door bore the name of "Miss

Muncey, milliner," and I sometimes did meet
lank and lymphatic young women on the stairs, I
had to infer that the third-floor—the garrets, in
fact—constituted the work-rooms and show-rooms
of Miss Muncey.

The little sitting-room occupied by the Brauns
was perhaps as poorly-furnished an apartment as
any could well be which did not proclaim actual
destitution. A few of the poorest cane-chairs, and
not more than a few; an arm-chair, covered with
the cheapest flowered calico; a central table of
deal, with a faded, over-washed cover; these and
an infirm sofa made up the principal part of the
stock of furniture. There was, however, a piano
of good tone—a relic of better days—with which
Christina would not part, and which indeed was
her sole capital and "plant" as a musician. There
were always flowers in the room, and botanical
specimens carefully pressed and tastefully displayed; there were two or three pretty vases of
Bohemian glass; there was Mr. Braun's flute,
really a handsome article, with old-fashioned
silver keys; there was his pipe, huge, and likewise silver-mounted: these and other stray pro-
perties gave an appearance to the room which at

least suggested refinement, and something like ornament. And I should not surely omit to mention a beautifully-carved and polished book-case, small, but of genuine oak and admirable workmanship; and I knew the moment I saw it whose hand had wrought it, and whose gift it was. "It was given to my father," said Christina to me afterwards, "not to me. I would not have taken it, though I know poor Ned would have been vexed by a refusal, and so I am glad he didn't offer it to me."

It was easy to understand, after an evening spent in this little room, why the burden of life had fallen so heavily and so early upon my poor Christina. Her father had entirely given up all idea of struggling any longer with the world, although he was far from being too old for stout and stiff exertion. He was the gentlest and the feeblest being I ever met. He was a small, very small man, with a pale, thin, clearly-marked, handsome face; a benevolent, mild, and placid expression; soft, silky, scanty gray hair; and large, dark, gray-blue eyes. His eyes were precisely like his daughter's, much darker than his complexion would have led you to expect; but

there the resemblance ceased. Mr. Braun spoke
English admirably; he played the piano and the
flute well; he was an accomplished botanist, and
knew a good deal about chemistry and astronomy.
He talked much of flowers, of stars, of the poetry
of nature, of shadows and sunrises, of beautiful
and gentle things generally; and of the poets and
writers who sang and discoursed of such things.
When he was not playing his flute, he commonly
sat and smoked his pipe, the bowl of which rested
on the ground, all the evening through. He
always rose early, and walked on the hills or by
the sea; rose none the less early though he had
been out on the strand watching some planet or
constellation till long past midnight; and while
Christina provided him with the means of living,
he repaid her with fresh flowers, and observations
on the heavens, and the beauty of life, and the
divine purpose in everything. He was, indeed, a
thoroughly-impracticable, well-meaning, good-for-
nothing, lovable old man. He would have pro-
voked me terribly, I think, if I were his son; but
he did not seem to provoke Christina. She appeared to take it as quite a matter of course that
her father should smoke his pipe, or botanise,

while she toiled to get money and provide dinner, and make the two ends meet. He was always sweet, mild, and happy. He had been blessed, or cursed, with that calm, light nature which can put away trouble or responsibility in a moment, and find enjoyment anywhere. He had lost wife and children—six children—all of whom he dearly loved; but he lived on tranquil, and spoke of them as having been happily transferred to amaranthine bowers, where they had only to await his coming. What he had himself done to merit that sure translation to immortal bliss, I never could learn; but it was clear that his mind was quite made up on that point. So, too, of his daughter. She reverenced in him, as pure and lofty religious feeling, that which I always regarded merely as the physical placidity of a temperament not susceptible of any strong or keen emotion. An innocently-selfish, mildly-egotistic man, you could not help loving him, and I at least could not help sometimes despising him. While the stars shone, while the flowers bloomed, when the snow covered the ground and the frost made the brambles look like sprays and spars of crystal, he was happy, and could not be otherwise. He could forget hunger in the contemplation of a flower; all humanity in the polishing of a stone. He cared as little for active thought as for active pursuits; and knew less of politics than an American infant generally does. The political agitations, struggles, sufferings, aspirations of his own countrymen, inspired him only with a tranquil scorn. He often asked, with utter contempt in his tone, what it mattered who owned the Rhine, so long as men could see its waters shining as brightly as ever in the sun, and darkening as before in the shadows of the everlasting hills.

"German unity!" he would say scornfully, "Germany has unity. Has she not Goethe and Novalis and Jean Paul; has she not Fichte? Hapsburg owns not less Kant than Brandenburg; Bavaria can sing the songs of Uhland and Arndt, as well as Suabia. Our unity is in our soul, and our language, and our worship of the beautiful and divine. The rest is nothing — no, nothing at all, or mere smoke and cloud veiling the glow of the heaven, as Faust himself has said."

Mr. Braun never looked one moment beyond the present, and was angry in his mild way with anyone who did. He was displeased with Christina for singing of nights in the Cave of Harmony, not because he had any objection to the place, or the company, or the kind of life to which it introduced her : not because it overtasked her, or threatened to wear out her voice, or endangered her in any way; but because she had to leave him for some hours every evening, and he was lonely without her. So he was vexed with her, and chafed in his own small way, and was jealous, as if her leaving him was a wilful act of neglect, or indifference to his happiness. He did not concern himself to think who would pay the rent if poor Christina had not always had spirit and sense enough to act for herself. A sort of philosopher, he was perhaps wise in his own conceit of life's theory and purpose ; but philosophers of that school ought never to have any children. I have often thought that when Morality blames Rousseau for having abandoned his children to a foundling hospital, it blames him for one of the only wise things he ever did. Better to confide them to the care of any institution, managed by any sane and human creatures, than to keep them under his own melancholy and imbecile charge.

I took lessons in German from Mr. Braun.

I really wanted to learn the language, partly for its own sake, and more because it was Christina's native tongue. But of course my chief reason was to have a plausible excuse for coming often to the house. After the lapse of a quarter I paid him some money. He took it passively, and laid it beside him. Christina coming in soon after found the money, made inquiry about it, and gave it back to me. I would have resisted, but she flushed so angrily that I pocketed it without further objection.

" My father knows nothing about money," she said, " and never did. I arrange all that; it is good-enough task for women. *He* was made for something much better, and we always liked to spare him. I know he never meant to take any money from you; *you* have lost enough by us already."

For she would insist upon regarding my withdrawal from the choir as a high, mighty, and chivalrous sacrifice.

" You took this in mistake, father ?" she said, appealing to him; " you were not thinking; you took it, not observing ?"

" *Versteht sich*," he placidly replied, waving

away with his hand a cloud of smoke, and solemnly indifferent to the whole business. I said no more, and what future lessons I received were accepted without talk of payment.

I do not know what was the special charm which made me so suddenly fall in love with Christina Braun. Falling in love is indeed the most exact description of what befell me. From a smooth level of calm indifference I literally fell into a glowing deep of love. Nor did this condition seem likely to change. It was impossible for me not to continue loving her. To begin with, she was intensely, exuberantly, and above all things, feminine. In every glance and movement she now seemed to my opened eyes to diffuse some vague sense of womanhood all around her. As one is conscious of the presence of flowers which he does not see, as one feels the air surcharged with electricity before the thunderstorm, so I always felt the influence, the sensuous influence if you will, of idealised womanhood when Christina was near. I do not know whether this sort of feeling can be made intelligible in any words of mine, but I cannot better describe the sensation of delight, refinement, and romantic love which her mere presence awakened in my soul. As I look back now, all the purple light of youth, all the glamour of poetry, all the bewitching illusions of music, seem to glorify that time when first Christina's presence grew a familiar influence to me.

There was an extraordinary quality of quiet energy in her which amazed me when I came to appreciate it. It was not the energy which fusses and bustles—to most young men a terribly disenchanting and disagreeable quality. It was an energy which made itself silently felt: a great self - sufficing quality. The early necessity of thinking and acting for two, the impossibility of consulting with one who was as useless for consultation as a baby, had doubtless forced this quality into regular action. Christina seemed to be of that class of women who can make something almost out of nothing. For easy and prompt adornment of her graceful figure she had a positive genius. I have often wondered and admired to see what a splendid simulation of imposing concert-costume she could confer upon herself with a little white muslin and a few scraps of ribbon and roses; and she could put on an old

shawl in a style that Lady Hamilton might have
envied.

I grew into the habit of spending every dis-
engaged hour — and nearly the whole of every
Sunday — in the familiar little room over the
watchmaker's and under the milliner's. We
sang, we played, we read, we recited, we talked
German, we had very, very humble and modest
suppers : we were immensely sociable, uncon-
strained, full of sentiment, full of laughter, and
happy. Edward Lambert came sometimes and
took lessons on the flute from Mr. Braun, for
which I know he contrived delicately to make
some return in one way or another. A patient,
manly creature, he sometimes spent his whole
evening at his flute-lesson, while Christina and I
talked or sang duets on the nights when she was
free. I knew that he loved her, dearly and dis-
interestedly, without selfishness and without hope.
I knew that she regarded him as one might regard
a fond and faithful Newfoundland dog. After a
while he ceased to come very often, and when he
did come he talked chiefly to Mr. Braun.

These were pleasant times, and free. They
gave a sort of mild foretaste or breath of the Bohe-

mian life which awaited some of us. Whatever of
intellectual culture I have ever had, I owe its development to these days and evenings, to that mild
old man, to that girl. I learned to read French and
Italian and German, and to speak these languages
fluently enough, if not always very gracefully and
grammatically. Years and years after, a French-
woman told me I spoke French like a German
and not like an Englishman. A more happy,
harmless life no youth could well have spent.

Was I very much grieved when Ned Lambert
left our little circle and went away to London?
This happened when the kind of life, blended of
Arcadia and Bohemia, which I have been describing, had lasted nearly a year. Well, I parted
from the good fellow with a pang; but I must as-
suredly have felt relieved when he went away. He
was an ambitious young fellow enough; and his
ambition was to become something like an artist.
Therefore he made up his mind to be an organ-
builder; and a chance opened for him through
some friends in London, of which he willingly
availed himself. I happened just to come in to
Mr. Braun's on the day when Lambert was taking
his final leave. He was holding in his hand a

little purse, a parting keepsake from Christina, and twisting it awkwardly between his fingers.

"When shall we three meet again?" I began, endeavouring to say something pleasant.

"We three?—we four!" interjected Mr. Braun. "I am not to be left out of the prospect. I hope to be at the next meeting too."

"It must be in London, then," murmured poor Ned disconsolately. "I sha'n't come back here ever again—ever again."

The last time I saw Lambert—not long since —he told me that through all the intervening years he never did return to the old town, and never would.

"In London, then," said I; "for London we are all bound. We are not going to stop in this old place all our lives, while Ned Lambert becomes a great man, and makes a fortune in London."

"I'm not likely to come to much," said Lambert; "and I don't want to make a fortune—now."

I saw tears sparkle in Christina's eyes.

"Good-bye, Edward," she said; "but not for ever! O no, not for ever. You have been kinder and better than a brother to me for ever so long; and I shall never, never forget you."

She put her arm over his shoulder, drew him down towards her, and kissed him twice. Then she turned and went abruptly into her own room. Ned Lambert tossed his hand in the air as a kind of silent parting salute to us, and in a moment we heard his rapid steps descending the stairs.

"He is a good lad, Edward Lambert," said Mr. Braun; "a kind, true-hearted boy. He does remind me of some of our German youth, with his large grave face, and his strong hands, and his soft heart. He is fond of Christina; and he did ask her to marry him—ach, Gott, yes! and last night again. But she could not love him in that way, Emanuel. She could not love him to marry him, as *you* know." And the kind old man looked at me with beaming, gentle eyes.

Yes; I did know it by this time. I must have been stupidly undeserving of any woman's regard if I had not felt before now that Christina Braun loved me.

CHAPTER V.

NONE of us liked the singing-saloon. Not that there was anything bad about it except its name; that, in a small country-town, was quite enough. In our town it did not much matter whether a man, woman, or institution was really bad or good. The sole question was whether he, she, or it had a bad name. So it had long been our object that Christina should abandon the music-hall, and try to live by teaching singing and the piano. At last we resolved that a day-school should be opened. Yes; Mr. and Miss Braun's school—French, German, and music. We advertised in the local paper—rather a stretch of boldness on our part in those quiet days—and I brought in a copy of the paper that same evening, over which we gazed and laughed a good deal. Young ladies and gentlemen were to be taught;

and of course perfectly-original plans were to be adopted in the teaching of everything. A great brass-plate was got and engraved with the legend, "Mr. and Miss Braun's School." I crossed the street furtively to look at it, and report as to the effect; and the thing was so far accomplished.

Not many pupils came at first. The story of Christina's nightly performances had of course got abroad, and made mammas feel shy of such an instructress. Gradually, however, a few were got together, all from the humbler ranks of our middle plateau; these brought more; and the terms being moderate, and a good deal taught for the money, things began to look a little more prosperous.

Still, this was clearly not the kind of field which Christina's ambition would have sought. We had often indulged and talked over wild hopes that at some distant period we might sing together, *prima donna* and *primo tenore*, upon some great stage, with half a metropolis for our audience. "I saw Rubini," Mr. Braun would sometimes repeat, "in Italy, when he was your age— *ja wohl*, I knew him too,—and he had not a finer voice. No; that had he not." I report this eulogy of my voice without a blush. The tribunal which is proverbially wiser than Voltaire has since decided, very conclusively, that my voice is not quite equal to Rubini's. But at the time the praise was spoken it had some effect upon me other than to make me smile.

In fact it had become gradually understood that the musical and other fortunes of Christina and myself were to be associated in life and for life, whenever fate and favour should allow us to begin the struggle together. We were to make a great name in Florence, in Paris, in London. I need not say that we did not pause to consider whether any difficulties were likely to arise in the way of a pair who began by getting married as a preliminary to seeking their fortune. As to our solitary counsellor, he would have seen no objection whatever to any scheme which seemed graceful, disinterested, and somewhat romantic; and even if the scheme had none of these recommendations, he would have become reconciled to it or anything else in a quarter of an hour. So far, then, the common obstructions to the course of true love did not, in our case, rise to disturb the smoothness of the current. There were only three persons in the world to be consulted, or who cared a straw about the matter, and they were quite in harmony on the subject.

At least we were quite in harmony so far as the love and the main wish of two lives were concerned. But the feelings of Christina and myself did not always flow in the same channel. She was a true-born artist; I never was, except in the merely technical sense, an artist at all. She would have given up a fortune for a lyric success; if I were assured of an easy income, I should no more have thought of becoming a professional singer than of becoming an amateur fireman. Moreover, all her plans and projects now were for splendid success under my leadership. Like all women who have any imagination, she saw her lover as a hero destined to triumph on every field he chose to enter. She always arranged the plan of the future as if we could not fail. I looked forward with a secret dread of failure to every undertaking in which I was likely to bear a part. For all that is talked of man's idle self-conceit, I think an ignoble distrust of our own capabilities is one of the commonest of masculine weaknesses. In my case, indeed, my distrust was well justified in one sense; but it helped, more than anything else, to

spoil some part of my life. Christina really knew
what she could do; and she was only waiting for
the time to do it. She was quite happy, cooking
her father's sausage, and lighting his pipe; but
all the time she knew herself an embryo *prima
donna*, and regarded the musical world as only
waiting for her. There were times when I felt
something like a pang of pity for her inexperience,
and her confident, sanguine nature. I ought rather to have pitied my own inferior courage, miser-
ably-inferior endowments, inferior organisation altogether. Knowing what she became—knowing
what, under brighter auspices, she might have
become—it now seems to me the very blindness
of affection which made her dream for a moment
of placing herself and her career under the guidance and guardianship of one so miserably un-
worthy.

I often wondered how, with her ideas and her
hopes, she could have endured singing in a vulgar provincial music-hall. I told her as much.

"I would sing anywhere," she said, "rather
than be in debt. Father could do nothing, and
I must use every power I have, or he must starve.
I would have sung my songs in the streets rather

than see him troubled to get bread. So little
makes him happy, that it would be a shame if he
were to want anything; and then he is old, and
he remains not long, perhaps;" and tears stood
in her eyes. "I sang in a concert-saloon in Cologne, a room near the theatre; I wonder if it's
there now? I could find it in a moment, if I
were there; *we* will go there one day and look at
the outside of it; but only the outside, for I
hated the place itself. Yes, I sang there when
I was a little one,—yes, only ten years old."

"But you were not born in Cologne?"

"No, no; much farther away from this—across
the Vistula." (She mentioned an old historic
Prussian town.) "We only came to Cologne
when we were coming to England; and we only
came to England to go to America. But father
has not the art of getting forward in anything;
and so we remained a whole year in Cologne on
our way to England, and now we have been many
years in England on our way to America; and I
don't suppose we shall ever get there, unless *we*
go there some day to visit your brother, Emanuel."

"But we shall visit your birthplace some day,
shall we not, dearest?"

"I don't know, Emanuel; I don't like to think of it. I was not happy there—O, not happy at all, but very miserable; and I do not want ever to see the place any more. It is like a discord, or a broken string, or a harsh note, or something of that kind, coming into some beautiful delicious piece of music, when I turn from now to then. It was all so dull, and without colour, and sad and harsh. My father and brother never could agree." (I should mention that I was aware of one of Mr. Braun's sons being still alive.) "Louis was very harsh to father, and not forbearing. I don't remember what it was all about; but I can guess now that Louis thought—well, I suppose he thought my father had not been very prudent or persevering; but I know he was harsh, and he scolded, and his wife scolded. She was very cold and hard and religious, and she always scolded me. One day, I remember, she told me I had too great an appetite, and ate too much for a little beggar-girl; and I cried half the night through, and then got up and tried to steal away, to drown myself from one of the old bridges. But an old night-watchman found me,—I remember him so well; he had a horn and a spear of some kind,—and he brought me back; and she beat me, and I so hated her! At last father said he would go away, and I was delighted. I did not care where we went—anywhere, so that we went away. Louis indeed was not bad, for he gave us money to go; and she was not bad either. I think she must have been a good woman, but hard; and then she had children of her own, and we were mere dependents. So I came to sing in Cologne, Emanuel, and then here; and so ends my long, long story."

During the whole of the story, which she told in a dreamy kind of tone, her eyes and lips had marked its incidents with the symphony of deep expression. She lived the old life quite over again, as she thus ran it through for me. I was glad when the story was done, so painful was the emotion it had evidently caused her.

"How happy for me, dearest Christina, that you did not go to America! I only wish I had known you sooner, and were rich for your sake, and you should never have sung in a wretched saloon."

"I sang very badly in the place here lately; but I think it was because the people there knew nothing about singing, and there was no use in trying to sing well."

"You sang only too well for me; you bewildered me. I never heard such singing before—indeed, I never heard *any* singing before, in the true sense."

"Ah, I always sang my best when you were there. I saw you the very first night, and sang for you. I loved you even then, Emanuel, though I thought you came with no good will to me. Was I not angry and rude? *Ach!* I think I loved you always, before even that night,—yes from the very first."

"And will always, to the very last?" I whispered.

"Always,—O, always,—if you remain still what you are, what I believe you to be. And if not, then—"

"*Then*, dearest?"

"Then all my light will go out, Emanuel, and I shall be miserable for ever. O, if I ever think you do not love me beyond everything in this world, then I shall hate you—no, I don't believe I ever could hate you; but I shall be wretched, and perhaps make both of us unhappy for our

lives. But I think that you will never change;
I knew from the very first that you would some
time come to love me; and now I know that you
will love me always. Ah, how bright life is now!"

Her eyes sparkled in tears. We were alone
at this time in the little old room. She seated
herself at the piano and sang one of her German
hymns with even more than her wonted passion
of pathos. I sat listening in the deepening twi-
light of the calm summer evening, happy—tran-
scendently rapturous and happy.

Those were bright days. I have lingered long
over them here, although they sounded but as the
overture of my life, and really formed no part of
the drama itself. I have lingered over them, because they were so happy and because they were
so brief.

How long might we have gone on thus peace-
fully and happily, content with merely playing the
prelude of real existence? When should we have
married, and begun the business of our life-drama
in good earnest? These are speculations which
I used to be fond of going over and over in my
mind, but which I can hardly expect anybody else
to follow with interest. I dismiss them here from

my pages; but the words I have written may remain, for they will serve to indicate thus early that the drama was never played out as we had prearranged it.

The first discordant note which Fate struck in was the death of Christina's father. The mild old man passed suddenly but very quietly out of life. One evening he complained of having a headache and cold feet. When I came that night a doctor was with him. I remained all night. Whatever malady had seized my poor old friend kept a firm hold. Towards morning he talked a good deal, now in English, now in French, now in German, intelligibly but not coherently, of his early home, his wanderings, his lost wife (whom now he saw in Christina), his family one by one, his flowers. He murmured stray scraps of German poems: "Ueber allen Gipfeln ist Ruh"—those exquisite, mournful, consoling lines which came from Goethe's soul and hung late upon his dying lips; and he whispered now that he was going to learn all the secrets of the Creation; and he repeated faintly two lines from Uhland:

> "Da sind die Tage lang genug,
> Da sind die Nüchte mild."

Towards the end he brightened up into clearer consciousness, and called Christina by her name. I remember with a peculiar pang how he touched Christina's hand and then mine, smiled upon us in the old gentle way, full of trust and serenity, and so died. He looked only a little paler and milder in death than in life.

After this came a long sad interval, sweetened, I must own, to me by the consciousness that my presence and my love must be still more needful to Christina than before.

CHAPTER VI.

THE same little room, unchanged save for the absence of one of its old inmates, whose flute, pipe, and books stood untouched in their familiar former places. Christina and I were alone. We had been talking long and earnestly. She arose and went to the window, and looked silently and thoughtfully into the soft summer night-air. The breath of an exquisite day still haunted somehow the very pavement of the street below, and seemed to soften the hum and the tread of the people who passed under our window. The stars were faint in the violet sky, from which the light of day had not yet wholly faded.

Christina remained for a while motionless and silent, one hand keeping back her hair, the other arm resting on the side of the open window. This was one of those evenings at the close of summer when the dusk seems to descend suddenly like a veil; and as I looked admiringly and lovingly on her face, turned in profile to me and gazing westward, the roseate light which shone on it suddenly went out, and her cheek seemed pale and melancholy. As the room appeared to darken, she looked away from where the light in the west had been, and turned towards me smiling, with a sweet, sad expression, which I see even now.

"Emanuel," she said, "you have made me happy—happy, although we have lost my poor father. I never before knew what it was to feel even an hour's happiness. My life was always cold and hard, and I did not hope for much better on earth. Now I believe in happiness, for I believe in love. Do you know that I tried all I could to love poor Edward Lambert; he was so fond of me, and so good: but I could not. I did my best: I wished and prayed to love him, and I could not. I do not know what would have happened to me but for you. I know I never could have stayed with my brother in that place, which would be strange to me now. I think I should have had to find out the old bridge where I was going to drown myself before, and complete the work this time. What would have become of me if I had gone there?"

"What would have become of *me?*" I asked, with something of reproach at least in my voice.

"I don't know. I thought perhaps you would have been as happy without me,—but stop, don't scold me—indeed I don't think so now. If I succeeded in the world—"

"And didn't fling yourself from the bridge."

"And didn't fling myself from the bridge— don't laugh at me, that was quite a possibility too —if I didn't drown myself, but lived and succeeded, and made a great noise in the world, and got money, then you should have heard of me, for I would have come to you. If not, then you should never have heard or known anything more of me. I think that is what I meant to do, if I clearly meant to do anything. But you have changed all that, Emanuel, and it only remains—"

"It only remains to arrange our plans and to be happy."

"We will think of our plans to-morrow, when we are a little more calm and composed. All this has come on us rather suddenly, and I scarcely slept last night, Emanuel, with thinking of you, and how soon I must leave you. Then, even when I fell asleep at last towards morning, I

had such a horrid dream; I dreamt that you yourself, with your own lips, told me calmly I had
better go—that we had better separate; and I
awoke in misery. But that, thank Heaven! has
not come true, and I feel that we are acting the
wisest part. Life is not long enough for separation, is it, dearest? and I know my Emanuel will
not suffer loss in the end by his sacrifice. I see
the future all bright before us—as bright as the
sky was just now—that is, before the evening's
red had faded and the darkness come up."

Sacrifice! My sacrifice apparently was that I
consented to be loved as a man does not expect
to be loved a second time in this world.

Let me explain the source and meaning of the
conversation I have just described.

The death of Christina's father ought, in ac-
cordance with ordinary usage and respect for public opinion, to have somewhat changed the manner
of our intercourse; but it did not—I still spent
every evening with Christina as before. I sat
beside her while she made her mourning-dress;
I was beside her in the deepest of her affliction,
and in its gradual subsidence. When the funeral
had been long over, and the clergyman and one

or two other friends who came out of mere kindness had ceased to visit her, I came regularly every evening, and sat for hours with her just as before. I can say literally that all the time I did not give to business or to sleep I gave to her. I always left her with reluctance, though the separation was but for a few hours. I always hastened eagerly to her, although only a few hours had passed since our last meeting. We walked together of evenings on the hills and by the sea, and watched the line of light that streamed from the west until it seemed to fade into the waves and the night and the stars came up. I learned from her to know each constellation that lights our northern horizon. Her father had taught her, like himself, to live among the stars and love them. I loved to hear her talk as much as to hear her sing—ay, "far above singing." My whole nature was quickened and purified by hers; it was the old, old story of Cymon and Iphigenia over again.

Of course it must have been dreadfully improper, not to say dangerous, thus to spend long evenings after evenings together and alone. But we never thought it so, and indeed never thought about the matter at all. I know that nothing

could have been purer than our love, more innocent than our intercourse. I do not recommend
that sort of thing as a rule—I see all the danger
of it; I see that the two very best people in the
world—and we, good lack, were not even the
second-best—might have found reason to repent
such heedless self-confidence. But it is certain
that we trod the furnace unscathed—nay, that
we did not even know we were girt with fire from
which ordinary eyes would say there was no es-
caping. I do not well know what preserved us;
perhaps our very unconsciousness of danger, perhaps poetry, perhaps music, perhaps sentiment-
ality, perhaps that generous subtle fire of youthful
love which has so little of the animal oil in its
composition. I can only say that, when we were
driven out of our terrestrial paradise, we had at
least no cause to blush, or hang our heads, or
cover ourselves, because of shame.

Of course, however, this was not the view of
the matter taken by our neighbours. It was not
likely that in such a miserable little town, en-
slaved by the judgment of Mrs. Grundy, conduct
like ours could escape gossip and criticism. The
people living in the same house with Christina

knew of our meetings; pupils of Christina's called occasionally in the evening and found us together; many good-natured persons began to talk about us, of whom, I can say in all sincerity, we had never conversed. This kind of talk must at last reach Christina's ears; and it did.

One evening when I came as usual I was told that she was not at home; and I was much surprised, knowing how few acquaintances she had, and how little she cared to visit any of them. The next evening the same thing occurred. The next day I wrote her a letter asking, somewhat warmly, for an explanation. I received a reply full of love and tenderness, begging of me not to come that evening, but promising to write again. I did not grow jealous, or suspicious, or angry. I knew that Christina's heart lay open to me; but I became alarmed, expectant of some evil news; restless, sad. I think I had from the beginning a foreboding that something disagreeable would reach us from her brother. Immediately on poor Mr. Braun's death Christina had written to her brother, acquainting him with the event, describing exactly and frankly her own position and prospects, and asking simply for any advice he could give. For weeks no answer came; but we were not much surprised. In those days railways did not traverse East Prussia and connect Ostend with St. Petersburg.

At last I received a little note from Christina, written in apparent haste, and asking me to see her that evening. I went at the earliest possible moment. It was the evening with which this chapter opens.

I hurried upstairs, and found her door open. I went in, and saw her alone, kneeling on the floor, and engaged in packing up some clothes, books, and music. She looked up, and there was so sad an expression in her face, that I positively started.

"Christina, my dearest," I said, kneeling on the ground beside her, "what on earth has happened? Why do you look so sad—and why would you not see me before?"

"I am going away, Emanuel," she replied, in a very faltering voice.

"Going away! Going where? Away from me? No, that I know you are not."

"Ah, yes; it is quite true. I am going to Reichsberg—I must go!"

"Never! you shall not!"

"I must, indeed. See, Emanuel, here is my brother's letter. Read what he writes."

I took the letter and tried to read it. It was in German, written in a dreadful character, which danced before my eyes maddeningly. After some impatient bungling efforts, I thrust it into her hand.

"Read it, Christina," I said; "and let me know the meaning of all this, for Heaven's sake!"

She read me the letter. It was long, well-meaning, cold but not unkindly, intensely moral, pious, and philistinish. It expressed well-regulated regret for the death of Mr. Braun, but it made it a duty to allude rather pointedly to his faults and his weaknesses. It showed how these faults and weaknesses had now left the daughter whom he, the father, so professed to love, homeless and unprovided with any means, at scarcely nineteen years of age, in a far-off foreign country. It expressed a hope that Mr. Braun had found in dying that spiritual comfort and faith which he ostentatiously rejected during his lifetime.

All this I listened to somewhat impatiently as Christina put into half-intelligible English its long sentences. But the point of the story lay

in the concluding passages, and these soon se-
cured my whole attention. Louis Braun disap-
proved and deplored the kind of life his sister
had led as a singer, utterly demurred to her idea
of ultimately going on the stage, and enjoined,
nay insisted on her immediately leaving England
and placing herself under his protection. He
enclosed some abominable Prussian notes for the
purpose of assisting her to undertake the journey,
which he recommended her to make by way of
steamer or sailing-vessel from London or Hull to
Dantzic.

"It's kind of Louis," Christina stammered
out when she had read to the end. "You see,
Emanuel, he has a good heart, and means for
the best. I can do nothing else. I must go;
and I will help him in his business, and attend
to his shop. But I will go on the stage and sing
yet one day, for all that."

"You shall not go to him!" I exclaimed.
"You shall be the servant of no brother, and
attend to no shop. What right has your brother
to control you? What has he ever done for you,
that he should attempt to order you about in that
way? What account of your movements have

you to render to him ? Leave it to me ; *I'll* write to him."

" Louis knows not one word of English ; and, dear Emanuel, I don't think your German would be quite certain to explain itself clearly to him."

" Now, I know you don't think of going," I said, warmly clasping her ; " you never could smile in that way if you thought of leaving me. Write yourself, then, and tell your brother that he may go—I mean that when you really needed his protection he did not offer it, and that now you don't want it, and will have none of it. No, don't write that—of course you would not—but write and tell him you will not and cannot go."

" But what can we do, Emanuel ?" she asked, looking up at me with her large eyes, now all sadness and seriousness. " My brother's letter is not all ; but my pupils—I did not like to tell you before—are all dropping away. Yes, it is quite true ; soon, I fear, I shall have none. The people here talk so much ; and now they talk of us, who never did them any harm. Yesterday a lady who had always been my good friend took away her three girls. After the holidays, some always do not come back ; and this time I shall

have very, very few. I met Miss Griffin a week
ago, and she spoke very strangely and coldly to
me. I do not care about my brother much—
I hardly know him at all; but I see that I had
better go to him, and even for your sake I must
go; and perhaps—O, perhaps, my own dear
Emanuel—we may meet once again."

"Once again! We will never part—never!
Why cannot we at once put a stop to the talk
of all these people? Why cannot we be married now—to-morrow? We do not want much
to make us happy. Listen, Christina—hear what
a salary I have; in a place like this we might
live on it for ever;" and I whispered its amount
—about as much as a fast young Londoner might
spend in gloves and cigars.

Christina made no answer. Was she over-
whelmed by the largeness of my means, or rendered aghast by their smallness?

"We shall be the happiest people in the
world," I urged. "You can give music-lessons,
if you like; or we will give concerts together.
Why, the singers at that concert in the Assem-
bly Rooms last night were good-for-nothing hum-
bugs, I have been told; and yet people paid to

hear them just because they came from London.
I am sure no one of them had a voice anything
like yours. We only want to get known. We
can't give musical entertainments together now,
that's quite clear; but Mr. and Mrs. Emanuel
Temple Banks would sound famously, *nicht wahr?*"
said I, endeavouring to become jocular. " Or
suppose I come out as a blind singer, like Vult,
in the story—Richter's story—your poor father
read to us so patiently when we were not listening
to half of it? Suppose I be a blind singer, and
you my wife or sister, sustaining and guiding
me? I think it would draw splendidly."

" Nonsense, Emanuel; you must not talk
such nonsense," said Christina, smiling never-
theless, though perhaps a watery smile. " We
cannot be married yet, it would be too rash;
and what would people say?"

" What should we care? Let them say what
they please. It doesn't appear that the people
who concern themselves about us say such very
flattering things already that we need court their
good opinion. Let them speak well or ill of us
—there is a world elsewhere," I exclaimed, in
splendid Coriolanus fashion.

"There is, there is indeed, Emanuel!" she said, springing up and with brightening eyes; "there is a world elsewhere, thank Heaven! which is not like this narrow and miserable little place. O, who would live here and stagnate, when there are places where life has a chance of success!"

I saw that she was yielding, and I pressed my advantage. I clasped her in my arms, and vowed I would not release her until she had pledged herself never to leave me.

"How could I refuse any longer?" she said at last. "You have prevailed, my own; ah, I am afraid I was only too willing that you should prevail. If you are not unwilling to sacrifice yourself for a poor singing girl, what can she do but accept the sacrifice when she loves you so dearly as I do?"

It was then that she gently withdrew from me for a moment, and went to the window, as we saw her at the opening of this chapter. "Dost thou look at the stars, O my star?"

We spoke but little of our plans and prospects that night; we were too happy for talk. Strange thing in mortal life, we knew we were happy! It is not retrospect alone which throws for me a

golden glory round that unforgotten evening; I
knew at the hour that a golden atmosphere floated
round us both.

Christina had utterly flung away the early
doubt and despondency of the evening, and returned to the old joyous self-confidence. She
looked at the future with the brightest eyes.

"No chance of our failing, Emanuel," she
said ecstatically.

"And even if we do fail, my dearest," I replied, "what then? We shall be none the less
happy. I do not care one rush for any success
in life while we can live for each other and be
happy. We only value life itself that we may
love each other and be happy."

She smiled a triumphant smile. "Have no
fear," she said; "we shall have love and happiness and success too. I know we shall; I see
the future as clear as to-day. Now, dearest, you
must go. I shall see you to-morrow night, shall
I not?"

Needless to give my answer—rather, I should
say, to describe it. As I was leaving, my eye
fell upon the trunk which she had been packing
when I came in.

"You may undo your work of packing now, *liebchen*," I said smilingly.

"Nay, is it worth while?" she asked, smiling with a significance I did not understand. "Remember the world elsewhere."

Need I say how we parted? Need I tell how often I walked backward and forward under her window that night? Need I say that I felt the happiest and the proudest of human creatures? Need I say how I lay awake, and tossed half the night through, recalling every word, every glance, every kiss; how I shaped out plan after plan for our future path of life; how I felt all the passion and the ecstasy, without any of the doubts and feverish fears and torturing pangs, of love?

CHAPTER VII.

I HAVE already said that the one thing which
gave me any uneasiness as to the future was
Christina's passionate desire to go on the stage.
This had not, indeed, been a discordant note in
our harmony; but it was one I always endeavoured not to touch. I kept the question as
much as I could out of sight; I compromised
with it, made myself believe it would arrange
itself somehow. In fact, I was afraid of it, but
still kept hoping it would come to nothing; for
the more and more I loved Christina, the more
and more I wished to keep her wholly to myself, the more jealous I grew of any art,
any profession, which could divide her thoughts
with me and my love. I could have lived in a
desert island with her for ever—yes, I still think
I could—and never wearied of her, or longed for
other companionship. Doubtless to most persons

such a profession will seem merely the conscious
or unconscious exaggeration of sentiment; doubtless in their case it would be so. I am speaking
of myself—of my own heart, and of what I know.
I could have lived with her—we two alone—a
long life through, and known no weariness or
change if she knew none. The first strong emotion of all my life was love for her; and the more
I grew to love her, the more jealous I became of
the art which she so loved.

I should have been glad to compromise for a
life of music-teaching and singing at concerts
and oratorios, and such milder and safer paths
of the lyric art. Indeed, I had myself had several engagements at local performances of the
kind, and was, as I have mentioned already, becoming a sort of small, very small, celebrity. I
was saving a little money to begin married life
withal, and was very economical and careful, my
whole heart being set on one object; neverthe-
less, the general impression of respectable and
good people in our circle still was that I was
simply going to the devil.

Now the attorney in whose office I daily
worked was a very respectable man. He was a

pious man, and sang very loud in church. He
was also a very pompous man. He had a very
respectable, pious, and pompous wife. He con-
sorted with the rector; he sometimes dined with
the local lord; and at the annual flower-show
his wife was always taken notice of and politely
spoken to by an evangelical countess, and by the
wives of the county members.

The very morning after I had made my pact
with Christina, I was summoned to my employer's
room almost immediately on his reaching the
office. When I came into the presence of Mr.
Bollington—that was his name—I saw, by the
very way in which he settled his neck into his
collar, that something was up. I may say that I
never liked Mr. Bollington; his manner somehow
seemed always to convey to me the idea that he
regarded a salaried clerk as simply a poor devil.

"O, ah, Mr. Banks," he began. "Yes; I
want to speak to you. Close the door. Thank
you; that'll do. Mr. Banks, I hear you are
getting very much into the way of singing at
nights at concerts and oratorios, and all that
kind of thing. Now, that is not quite a legal
sort of thing, nor quite respectable in our line

of business; and I am rather afraid it will tell against us, you know. I am very particular, Mr. Banks, as you know. Law is rather a particular sort of business. People say law is jealous, and won't have any rival, don't they? I think some poet or novelist, or somebody, says something of the kind. I don't think it will do, Mr. Banks; I don't indeed. Law is drier and duller than music; but I think you'll find it better in the long-run."

I was a good deal embarrassed by this address. I had no respect for Mr. Bollington; I knew him to be merely a stupid, respectable old ass; but respectability has somehow an awful sort of halo of divine right yet lingering about it, and it impresses the Bohemian more than he cares to acknowledge. I, an embryo Bohemian, had always to make a little mental struggle to assert myself against this respectable member of society. Now, however, there were other reasons to embarrass me; he seemed actually inspired with a purpose to destroy all my projects.

I stammered out something about being fond of music, and not seeing any harm in such devotion.

"Pardon me; I have not said there was any harm. A taste for music is very respectable; and I am the last man in the world likely to find fault with an inclination which some of the most respectable persons I know, even in my profession, cultivate,—in a manner which, in fact, adds to their respectability, I may say. But that is in an amateur way, Mr. Banks; in an amateur way. It is quite different when one comes to be a professional performer; and I hear, Mr. Banks, that you have been going quite into the professional line of late. Now, you have not consulted me on the subject, or ascertained whether I considered such an occupation quite consistent with your position here; and I have therefore found it necessary to send for you, and—in fact, to open the subject myself."

"I really didn't suppose," I said, "that you could have any objection to my improving my income by any means—any honourable means, of course—which did not interfere with my character or my business here. I have not been inattentive to the office."

"Pardon me; I have made no charge of the kind."

"I do not see why one may not have different occupations at different hours of the day."

"In a general way there may be no objection. Many occupations admit of such combination; but we are now speaking of a particular case. This firm, Mr. Banks, has a character for strict attention to business, and business of a peculiar and exclusively respectable kind. I don't say that in a certain kind of low criminal business, for example, there is necessarily any reason why a solicitor should object to his clerk singing at concerts after office-hours. I think it quite possible that such singing and a certain kind of criminal business might combine very well. But ours is not a business of that class, Mr. Banks. Our clients are of quite a different order of life, and they have strong and very proper views on the all-importance of respectability."

"But really, Mr. Bollington"—I had now quite reasserted myself; stupidity had washed all the imposing gilt off respectability, and I could have laughed at or sworn at it—"really, Mr. Bollington, I don't quite see that I am bound to give up everything to such views."

"Not bound at all, Mr. Banks; certainly not

bound. You are not an articled clerk, and are quite free to act as you please. Let the conversation close for the present. Be so good as to think the matter over. I am sure you understand my determination. You can therefore decide for yourself, and let me know, and we can recur to the subject, if necessary, say the day after to-morrow. And now, Mr. Banks, about the papers in the case of Davys and Pontypool, if you please."

This was of course an *ultimatum*. A greater *contretemps* could hardly have occurred. All my plans for the present were based on that very combination of music and law which Mr. Bollington declared to be only possible, if at all, in the case of a very low sort of criminal business. This was a sharp and sudden blow to me; and I had the whole day to bear it before I could pour out my bad news and my feelings to Christina.

Grimly enough I went to her lodgings that evening. I thought the very sky looked gray above me; and Christina's gladsome confident eyes were a sort of new pang and reproach to me.

"O Emanuel, I am so delighted to hear it!" was the reply with which she broke out when,

with a sad face, I had got through my dismal
news. "I am delighted from my heart to hear
it! Why should you stay in so miserable a place,
and be paid a few wretched shillings a-week, you
who are better than them all; you with your voice
—and your talents—for you know I never would
care for mere voice. No; you are rid of it all
now, and are free. Now you will have to throw
your soul into the art you are fitted for, my dear
Emanuel. Ill news, dear! This is the best and
brightest of news to Christina. I always feared
that you would be content to work and wait here,
and I have had enough of working and waiting.
You are so easily contented—O, far too easily
contented; but only because you are modest of
your talents, and do not know what you deserve
and what you can be, as I do. No, no; my
Emanuel will be no more a slave, but an artist.
Tell him so, and be free."

There was something pitiful to me in hearing
the enthusiastic girl run on in this wild way.

"Alas, Christina," I said, "it is not so easy
to make a great way in the world as you think,—
you girls, with your vivid imagination and your
confidence. You see me with eyes which will

guide nobody else. Think how difficult it is to get on in this place."

"In this place! Yes; but who would think of this place? Leave it, my Emanuel! London and Paris—these are the places for us. Why delay here at all? why not go to London at once, and together? why, dearest Emanuel, why?"

Her impatience rose to something like wildness.

"Because, my love," I said, looking as wise and as cheerful as I could contrive to do, "because in London people who have neither money nor friends may have to starve."

"But we have some money. I have saved some; a little—and not so very little. See!"

And she showed me in triumph a few poor sovereigns heaped up in a drawer, where anybody who chanced to enter her room might have found, and, if so inclined, stolen them. I could hardly keep back my tears—I was only a boy, after all; and there was something unspeakably pitiful and touching in the pride and confidence built upon the few poor golden coins.

"My dearest, your money and mine would not keep us long in London. People must endeavour to make a beginning where they have friends."

" Then you are content to give up your career; give up your chance of becoming a great artist— as I know you would be?"

"No, not give up, my own Christina, but just wait only a little for a better chance. Listen, you wild girl; we must give up something—"

"But listen, Emanuel. I have set my very soul on being a great singer, and on your being one too. You may think me a mad creature; but I know that in this I am wiser than you. Don't stop on the way, and don't be afraid. I am not afraid; why should you—a man?"

"You are not afraid," I said, taking both her hands, and trying to pet her into calmness, " because you are a generous, imaginative, darling girl, who, once you love a man, think the world must see him as you do, and that he must turn out something great. I know more of the world, and of myself, than you do. I only ask that we should be patient for the sake of each other. I cannot do anything which might make you un- happy. You may be ready to sacrifice yourself; but don't ask me to sacrifice you."

"Listen, Emanuel," she said, disengaging her hands from mine, and then laying one arm on my

shoulder and looking earnestly, imploringly at me
(I see her deep dark eyes and eager trembling lips
even now this moment); "do not talk of waiting
and of patience, and of living a life of dull, stupid
plodding in this hateful place. Only last evening
you appealed to me—and persuaded me; let me
now persuade you. Do you think me bold to speak
in this way? Yes, I am bold now, because I love
you so, because you are all in the world to me,
and I tremble to think of our separation."

"Separation? Who speaks of separation?
What could separate us?"

"You do not know; I do not know; anything,
any delay—a night's reflection may change our
fortunes, may change our hearts! I tremble to
hear you talk as if you only wished to cling to this
place for ever."

"And I tremble to hear you speak as if ambition, and not love, were your impulse, Christina!
Yes, I could be happy with you here, even here,
for ever!"

"But let us not talk of that. I could not see
you condemned to an ignoble, stupid life here; I
love you far too deeply. Your ambition is mine;
your success would be mine. O Emanuel, love

me and my ambition too, or you cannot love me, you cannot understand me at all!"

"If the choice were between your love and your ambition," I said sullenly, "I know which would win."

"You can't divide them; they are one and the same. They are as my heart and my soul. O Emanuel, you know I love you. I have no one on earth whom I care for but you."

"And yet if it were a choice between giving up your chance of a career, your dream of a career" —I was now bitterly jealous of her ambition, and spoke in almost savage tones—"you would throw me away without a thought. Do you call that love?"

"No," she replied vehemently, and turning from me, "I do not. But I loved an ambitious man, a brave man, an artist, and not a slave."

Had she struck me in the face, I could not have felt the blow more heavily. A surprised, passionate, injured cry was breaking from my lips. I repressed it with all the force of energy I could call up; but I turned away, and, sitting on the nearest chair, covered my face with my hands.

I do not know how many minutes or seconds I

had sat thus. It seemed to me a long interval of bewildered pain and bitterness. I felt at last a hand laid on mine, and a sweet piteous voice murmured "Emanuel!" I allowed the hand that covered my face to be drawn away; and then I saw that Christina was kneeling at my feet, and looking up at me with eyes full of tears.

"O forgive me!" she exclaimed; "my dear, dear Emanuel, forgive me; I did not know what I was saying."

"You have cruelly misinterpreted me, Christina."

"I have indeed; and that is the second time in our lives I have done so. But I will do so no more. How could I use such cruel, shameful, false words to you! But I was disappointed; O, so bitterly disappointed; and I was mad."

"Dearest Christina, you know—if you do not, at least Heaven knows—that I only think of your happiness, that I only shrink from exposing you to utter poverty."

"But what else have I suffered from my birth? I am well used to poverty. Ah, if you did but know all! I prefer any poverty, even alone, to going to my brother. Why should I fear it with you? But I will not talk in that way any more; I was foolish and wild; and you were right not to heed my folly. You are calm and have sense, and you know the world."

"You are a true woman, a true heroine," I said, my bitterness wholly melted away by her sweetness and submission, "and you would rather have the courage which springs without counting the consequences than that which calculates and waits. So would I, perhaps, if the consequences only affected myself alone; but a man who has the happiness of the woman he loves placed in his hands must not plunge headlong with her and himself too. No, my dearest, the courage which endures is often the best. We can wait for our career."

"We must wait indeed, Emmanuel; and perhaps a long time. You must have thought me a wild, romantic fool. I am sorry now, for I see that you are right."

"Then I have convinced you?" I asked joyously, proud of my pitiful and jealous prudence, as if it were anything but faint-heartedness, suspicion, and folly.

"You *have* convinced me," she said, in a low,

sad voice. " Let us not speak of it now any more, Emanuel; at least for to-night. I will sing you something."

She sat down to her piano and sang, and I listened until the dusk deepened into night. We parted with affection; but there was a sadness in her manner which I might have thought ominous. As I stood a moment below her window, I heard her still faintly singing, and knew that she was not sitting, but moving through the room. I walked slowly away, often looking back; suddenly I heard her window raised, and, turning round, I could see, in the deep purple of a late summer night, the outline of her head and neck dark against the sky. I thought she beckoned to me, and I hurried back.

" Only to say good-bye," she said in a whisper; and she seemed strangely fluttered and excited. " I only wanted to say good-bye once more, dearest; just good-bye."

As she leaned from the window a rose she was wearing in her breast fell at my feet. I took it up and put it to my lips. Some coming footsteps were heard, and she whispered in a very faint, very sad tone the word " *Ade*." Then she quickly

closed the window and drew the curtain, and I
could see her no more.

Her voice lingered in my ears as I went slowly
home, and was in my dreams all night. I longed
for the next night, that I might listen to it
again.

So the next day dragged heavily through, and
I was impatient of it, of myself, of everything,
feverishly anxious to meet *her* again; haunted
fretfully by a fear that I had made myself look
mean in her eyes; by a doubt whether, after all,
my wisdom had not been folly; by a vague foreboding of disunion between us. I made many
mistakes and blunders that day; and Mr. Bollington more than once put up his double eye-
glass and looked at me with cold significant
scrutiny.

At last the hour came for leaving the office. I
was at the door, rejoiced to be free in the evening
sunlight; when a small boy, whom I knew well,
came up and handed me a letter. The urchin was
the youngest son of the poor watchmaker who had
the shop over which Christina lived, and he was
often bribed with buns, apples, and halfpence to
act as letter-carrier between us. So I knew at

once what he came for, and I snatched at his letter.

"O, but stop," said the young varlet; "is the office closed for the day?"

"Yes, Tom; what of that?"

"And you are home for the day?"

"Yes, yes. Why do you ask questions, you little imp?"

"Because she told me I wasn't to give it to you until you were coming away. I've had it in my pocket ever so long."

So he gave me the letter, and darted down the street, alternately whooping and whistling.

I opened it and read:

"My Well-beloved, Farewell! I have thought and thought, and I see we must not marry yet. O, forgive me, Emanuel, and be not so very sorry or lonely. I think we must not meet for a long time. I am gone away, and you must not think of following me or seeking me; for the Heaven has told me that now I could only be an encumbrance to you, and that if we were married now, you would be sorry one day. I go away that I may some time be able to help you. If ever I

can, then we shall meet again, for I will find you
and come to you. If not, then far better we meet
no·more. Either way it will be better, and you
will thank me some time, and say Christina had
right. I love you still; all the same as ever.
Still love me: farewell, and think of me often, as
I shall never, never forget you.

"CHRISTINA."

This was all. The letter was written in the
quaint half-German character and the constrained
foreign style which I knew so well. I turned down
a dark lane out of the sunny street; the ground
seemed to heave under my feet, and black spots
danced before my eyes in the sunlight. I was not
far from the sea—my old, old confidant; and I
hurried to it as if my lost love were to be found
by its margin. Staggering, slipping, with dazed
eyes and choking throat and bursting heart, I
reached the strand, and flung myself down, and
read the letter again and again and again. And
then I laid my head upon the ring of a rusty an-
chor, and I broke into a boyish passion and tem-
pest of tears. She had made her choice—and left
me! Of the beautiful happy life that had grown

up around us, and that seemed destined to live with our lives, there was nothing left me but my memory, my grief, my agony—a few letters, and the flower that last night had fallen from her breast.

From that time I never saw her face for ten long years.

Did I make any effort to recover her? Did I not? All I could learn at her lodgings was simply that she had gone by the London coach, and that she had said she was going to her brother's. I hurried up to London by the very next coach— with what result I need hardly say. Utterly a stranger in the metropolis, my search there was quite thrown away. I could only learn at the coach-office that such a girl had actually travelled to town the day before, and that was all anybody knew of her. I wasted days in hunting about the docks for Dantzic or Königsberg ships or steamers. I found nothing of her. Then I bethought me that she might have gone to Hull, and I too went to Hull; of course utterly too late to have stopped her even had she gone there. I had made up my mind to follow her, when it occurred to me that perhaps, after all, she had relented and written to

me some word of comfort and guidance, and I
hurried back to my native town. No letter awaited
me, and I resolved at least to try the last chance
and follow her to her brother's. I remembered
the name of the street in which her brother lived,
and it could not be difficult to find the house.
Besides, I was now seized with a detestation of
our town and all that belonged to it; and it
seemed to me that I must leave it or go mad.
The thought of living there without her, of toiling
there uncheered and unloved, of spending drear
evenings alone where I had been so happy, of
looking up at the window where she could no
longer be seen; all this was simply intolerable to
me. I had never entered my old employer's door
from the evening when I received Christina's letter. What Mr. Bollington thought of me, or
whether he thought about me at all, I cared nothing. I sent no explanation or word of any kind.
I had some little money saved; I sold some few
poor things, and got a little more money; and I
took a passage in a Baltic vessel which was to put
in at Dantzic. One fair sweet autumn evening I
looked back on the strand where I had read Christina's letter, and watched the white houses of the

old town of my childhood, and the hill whereon was my mother's grave, until all sank out of sight, and with them closed the first bright chapter of my life.

The weather changed, and we had a rough, slow, miserable passage. Our wretched heavy old tub was beaten about the North Sea and the Baltic so long that it seemed to me as if life had been actually changed into a perpetual tossing on broken wintry waters. At last we reached Dantzic, and I made my way to Christina's native town,—a town of canals and islands, and numberless bridges, and steep, narrow, darkling streets, with whole populations living in each house. I found Christina's people at last. They received me at first coldly, and even harshly, regarding me as her evil genius; but having at length come to understand that she had renounced me, they lapsed into pity and were kind. But they knew nothing about her—absolutely nothing. She had not come there; she had not written any reply to their last letter. My coming first told them that she had left her old home. My journey had been utterly fruitless and futile.

I took a passage again for England. Sick at

heart, and weak in frame, with only two or three sovereigns left, I landed one wet, foggy evening near the Tower of London. As I stepped ashore I said to myself, "Here, then, in London will I stay. I accept battle here. I will succeed here or fail. I will live here, if I can; if not, I do not much care how or how soon I am to die here. Here I shall meet Christina again, or nowhere."

CHAPTER VIII.

FROM ARCADIA TO BOHEMIA.

So I kept my word, and drudged for years in the solitude and darkness of London poverty and struggle. I gave myself up to the teaching of music and to concert-singing, when I could get a decent engagement, or indeed any engagement at all. Understand that mine was for a long time a hard struggle. I lived in a garret—I was familiar with hunger. The details of the first few years may be spared. Stories of struggles in London by rising young men have all a sort of family resemblance; indeed, they are as much alike as Lely's court beauties; and if they sometimes differ in catastrophe—one adventurous career ending in Westminster Abbey, and another in the Lambeth Workhouse—so one court beauty may have died in the purple, and another in the lazarhouse. I do not care to weary the reader with a minute account of my struggles for a living; I only ask him to understand that they were real and hard; that for a time they regularly included actual want; that they often meant destitution; that hunger was a common condition; that once or twice I thought it likely enough my fate must be to die of starvation. Let us pass over all this, and come to a time when I began to have a certain income, however small; when I had a few substantial engagements as a teacher of singing and music, and was beginning to think of struggling my way to Italy in the hope of returning thence a qualified candidate for a place on the lyric stage. For on this I had set my heart. Pride, disappointment, baffled love, all conspired to make this seem the necessary task of my life. To prove myself—even were it only to myself— not a failure, not a coward, was a resolution within me strong and tenacious as revenge. It was, indeed, my revenge.

I will not say that the memory of Christina had not somewhat softened, faded into a gentler recollection, during all this time. But its impression was always with me, giving sadness or courage, hope or despondency, as my chances and my mood would have it; always, most certainly, exalting and purifying the mournful monotony of my drudging life by the memory of something beautiful, tender, and distant. For years of my life I was in the habit daily of going up and down the river in the boats, and I became an intense admirer of St. Paul's. I admire that building— forgive me if the confession show stupidity and want of taste—more than Pantheon or Colosseum, than Westminster Abbey or Notre Dame, or Cologne or Antwerp Cathedral, or St. Pèter's or St. Sophia's. To look up at it from Blackfriars-bridge on a winter evening, when a cold heaven and a few whitening clouds are behind, and the dome seems a mere flat shape against the sky, a mere form and outline, delighted me. To see it sparkling in the rosy colour of a summer morning, with light and shade succeeding each other on its spires and its rounded sides, or rising out of the masses of sunset cloud-heaps like a glimpse of some glorious heaven-city, was a sight still more exquisite. Even when the November fog is around it, and its outlines can only be seen at broken and vague intervals, it is a delight to think that behind that curtain of vapour lie rich spires and domes which one breath of wind might reveal in all their beauty.

In whatever season or hour, it seems to me to romanticise and to sanctify the hideous commonplace stretch of roofs and chimneys, and wharves and the leaden Lethean river, on which it looks.   So was the memory of Christina, and the presence of my love and even of my disappointment, in my hard and commonplace life.

Sometimes I have deliberately come to one of the bridges in the early morning, and stood in one of the recesses and watched the different phases of beauty the glorious dome would assume in the glowing light and the changing clouds, until perhaps at last the whole air filled with brightness, and every cloud vanished, and the dome and cross were alone in the blue heaven.   But these were rare enjoyments.   Generally I caught glimpses of my favourite building as I made my way among the bustling crowds on the bridges or on Ludgate-hill, or as I passed beneath in one of the penny steamers.   So, too, of my memory of Christina. Sometimes I had an hour or a whole evening to give to my boyish love, and I brought her back before my mind and my eyes until she stood as clear and as lifelike before me as when we lived in Arcadia together.   But these, too, were rare delights. In ordinary life I only caught mental glimpses of her as I fought my way through vulgar difficulties, and obtained some mean and commonplace advantages. But the influence was there always. I am a believer in beauty and nature and love, and all the rest of it. With a memory like mine, a faint hope, a strong purpose like mine, life could never become wholly vulgar or contemptible. " So long," says the great prose-poet whom Christina's father used to read to us in the old nights, " as the sun keeps but the slenderest rim of its disc uneclipsed, the world is not given up to darkness."

All this time, be it understood, my ordinary way of life was very prosaic, poor, and mean. I was now—say seven years or so after my coming to London—only just lifting my head above mere poverty. I was utterly obscure. I was living in a low and swampy district on the Surrey bank of the Thames, in the Putney direction. I lodged there with a poor, respectable, and ladylike old person, whose appearance attracted me when I happened to come that way hunting for cheap and airy apartments. The neighbouring population consisted chiefly of brick-makers and market-gardeners. A park having been promised, a few rows of cheap stuccoed houses were built, and christened Albert-terraces, Garibaldi-villas, Almaplaces, and such other appropriate and attractive names as the whirligig of time chanced to bring within the easy intellectual range of speculating builders. The roads were damp and undrained, and the whole place looked specially cheerless. The inhabitants of the terraces, villas, and places in no case belonged to the indigenous population, but were of a half-genteel, half-pauper, and wholly nomad class, like ourselves. Many people tried letting lodgings or opening schools there, and failed. One or two persons having privately the care of insane patients, and probably rather anxious to keep them insane, brought them to bide in this dismal swamp. A few government civil officers—Customs, Inland Revenue, &c.—who had not risen in their departments, came and settled there. A forlorn water-colour painter, a hopeless photographer, were among our neighbours; in fact, any kind of people, who, dreadfully poor, yet would not wholly abandon the appearance of gentility, drifted thither naturally. So long as the villas and cottages were kept in decent repair,

they looked pleasant enough, and indeed rather
fine and imposing. A semi-detached villa with a
vast row of steps, and urns at either side, somewhat awed the visitor at first; but the urns were
full of dry mud and dead leaves and spiders; the
drawing-room was uncarpeted and hardly furnished; a dirty slatternly servant, or a little girl
with a torn frock and curl-papers, opened the
door; grass and weeds grew upon the sides of the
parapets; the only traffic consisted of great coal-
wagons going to and from the neighbouring rail-
way-stations. The lanes were blocked up with
perpetual mud; the frog looked in at the kitchen
window; the maggot and the worm made themselves free of the back-parlour. Here and there
small rows of shops had been begun, and suddenly
stopped, and no one ever seemed to have any idea
of completing them. My landlady's daughter
called the whole settlement " a refuge for the destitute." It was decaying, but not venerable; it
was new, but not fresh; it had all the disadvan-
tages of newness, and all the defects of age. I
heard a lady near whom I happened to sit one
evening in a river-steamer describe it to a companion, when its swampy flats came in sight, as

"a deathy place." The phrase was picturesque, effective, and very appropriate. It did look a deathy place; but it had the advantages—to me supreme—of being very cheap, and of having easy access to the river, and therefore to town. In this refuge for the destitute, then, began my march to wealth; in this deathy place opened my struggle for life.

My landlady and her daughter were poor—dreadfully poor. I had seen enough of poverty in my own town, and indeed in my own surroundings, but somehow it was not poverty like that of Mrs. Lyndon and her daughter Lilla. Provincial poverty is hardly ever indeed quite the same as London poverty—there is all the difference that exists between a thatched hovel and a Drury-lane garret. But that was not the difference here; Mrs. Lyndon was always clean, neat, and well-dressed; and she always seemed to be able to get mutton-chops for her daughter's dinner. The daughter always dressed like a girl accustomed to wear good clothes, and therefore not afraid to be occasionally shabby. She never looked worse than like a lady in dishabille. There was none of the artful neatness, the mournful nervous precision

of conscious poverty about her. What on earth
did they live on, that mother and daughter? I
had been with them now for a long time; I was
constantly being consulted by mother and daughter about their pecuniary affairs. I sometimes
counted over the amount which I knew the lodgers
to pay, and it still left a pound or two of the
house-rent unaccounted for, and the rates and
taxes altogether unapproached. Every other day
some tax-collector called and left a paper. These
documents used to lie in little dusty, sooty piles
on the chimneypiece; I do not know that Mrs.
Lyndon ever thought about attempting to pay off
any of them. I scarcely ever came in at the door
without seeing some collector arguing and threat-
ening in vain. I think the dwellers in these
neighbourhoods used to allow debts of this and
other kinds to run up until they reached an in-
surmountable pile, and then they removed at night
to another locality. They were up to all manner
of dodges. Sometimes the house was taken in
the daughter's name; and this fact enabled the
mother, who was always at home, to waive the
responsibility away from herself and stave-off the
collectors a little longer. They seemed ashamed

of nothing. Lilla would entertain me sometimes through a whole afternoon's walk with narratives of the straits to which they had been driven, and the success with which they had come through them. You could not contemplate poverty of this sort without an impression that in its meanness and its cynicism it bordered on vice, and yet its endurance, its frankness, its cheerful determination were dashed with a flavour of a kind of virtue. You must pity people so hard-up, and you must also feel a certain contempt for them; and yet in my case I could not help liking them, trusting in them, and feeling something resembling affection for them. They were in every sense so kind-hearted, in one sense at least so true; and then we were all so hard-up together, that mere necessity and propinquity made us companionable, as people may be who are forced to pass the night beneath the same tree in Hyde-park, or under the same dry arch of the Adelphi.

A girl like Lilla Lyndon was, to my provincial mind, a perfectly wonderful phenomenon. She was extremely pretty, with dark skin, and crisp wavy dark hair, and bright, laughing, twinkling eyes, and a smile the most confident, sweet, and

winning one could well be gladdened by. She had
plenty of talk, and she talked in a voice just a
little sharp, but with a charming accent; and in
whatever poverty and privation, she had something
like the manners of a lady. But these were not
the peculiarities which most struck me. I was
principally surprised by her inexhaustible knowledge of practical life. How old was she? Hardly
twenty, I should think, at the time I am now
telling of, and yet she seemed to know London,
its ways, its people, its life, its tricks and dodges,
high and low, to the very heart. No royal road
was that which had led to such learning! Many
a hard struggle must have been battled through
before such sad practical experience of the world's
warfare could be got into that pretty little curly
head.

Lilla always dressed with an appearance of
fashion. If a new style of bonnet came in, I
sometimes found her at night working away at
her own old bonnet, and next day it was converted
into a very deceptive imitation of the reigning
mode. She reconstructed her dresses as often as
the British Board of Admiralty reconstruct their
war-ships. When crinoline came in, she was in

the front of the fashion, with petticoats wide
enough for a duchess. She was always doing
some mending work to stockings and slippers.
She was absolutely without hypocrisy or deceit
of any kind; even the pardonable feminine de-
ception which keeps ready to hand a piece of
crochet-work or bead-ornamentation to be pro-
duced the moment a tap at the door announces
a visitor, while the real piece of work, the pair of
stays or flannel petticoat in process of repair, is
hastily thrust under the sofa-cushion. Whatever
Lilla Lyndon was doing when you came in, that
she kept on doing as unconcernedly as before.
You found her darning a stocking, perhaps, and
she continued the work—sometimes, it may be,
calling your special attention to the frayed and
tattered condition of the article. You found her
in curl-papers, and she volunteered the admission
that she was too lazy to take them out when getting up that morning, or that she wanted her hair
to be in particularly good curl that evening—
perhaps because her uncle was going to take her
somewhere. She was ashamed of nothing that
she did. Let me do prompt justice to a clever
and pretty girl, and say, to prevent my readers

from misjudging her, that she never did anything
to be ashamed of, except talk-over creditors, and
go in debt when she had no prospect of paying.
She was honest in every way except as regarded
creditors; and you could as easily have convinced
a cat that it is dishonourable to steal cream as
induced Lilla Lyndon at this period of her life to
believe that the laws of morality have anything to
do with the relations between debtor and creditor.

Lilla's uncle was for some time a mysterious
and mythical personage to me.   The very first
day I became acquainted with mother and daughter I heard of the uncle, who was a member of
Parliament, and had an estate in Leicestershire,
and who would not do much for them now, but
they hoped would do something some day for
Lilla.   They did not boast of him by any means
in the manner of ordinary poor people dragging-
in a story of a rich relation, but simply referred
to him as their one sole possible resource and
holdfast in utter emergencies.   Gradually I came
to hear of the various arts and expedients by which
Lilla contrived from time to time to coax or wring
a few pounds out of him.   Mrs. Lyndon never
ventured to go near him.   There was a sort of

treaty, I fancy, that she was never to intrude on him. I could gather from them that he could never forgive her for having been virtuous, and having thus rendered it necessary for his brother, when he fell in love with her, a poor girl, to marry her. He was now more angry with her than ever because she was poor and lonely, old and shabby. No doubt many of her shifts and schemes and pressing appeals for money often made the relationship seem a very discreditable thing. The mother and daughter had not known him very long. Lilla's childhood had been passed in Heaven knows what poverty and meanness, her mother never daring to apply to the wealthy and offended relative. Lilla herself told me, with some pride and much laughter, how she, being driven to utter desperation one day, determined upon hunting down her uncle, and how she found him out in his great house in Mayfair, and faced the powdered servants, and insisted upon seeing him; how she waited outside the hall-door for two mortal hours, very cold, very hungry, but resolute, and prepared for the encounter by being dressed in whatever finery she had got; how at last she saw him, and was rather gruffly received;

how she began to cry, thinking that the proper
way to soften a cruel uncle, but was soon unde-
ceived by the cruel uncle telling her sternly that
he hated crying women, whereupon she desisted
from weeping, the more readily because she had
not the least inclination to cry; and how at last
she compelled him to admit the relationship, and
came away with a permission to call again and a
ten-pound note. This present she changed at the
nearest shop, and treated herself forthwith to a
pair of gloves, a new bonnet, a fowl to be brought
home for dinner, and a hansom cab to her own
door.

Since then she had never lost sight of him.
He must either have begun to accept her existence and her visits as a kind of dispensation not
to be any longer resisted, or she must have really
succeeded, with her pretty face, genteel figure,
and coaxing ways, in making him fond of her.
He was a widower, and had daughters of his own;
but they would never see Lilla, who for her own
part was only too happy to escape seeing them;
and all her visits therefore were paid in the absence of these inflexible ladies. Mr. Lyndon
seemed to me, by Lilla's own admission, to have

done a good deal for her. He had obtained for
her situations as governess in various families in
London, in Cheltenham, in Edinburgh, in Bath,
in Scarborough ; but she always quitted her place
somewhat abruptly, and came back to her mother
revelling and rejoicing in her freedom, which she
celebrated by laying out part of the balance of her
salary in a fowl, or oysters, or a lobster, or something nice for supper. Terrible trouble had she
each time to make her explanations and excuses
to her uncle, and cozen him into forgiving her.
From various hints and stray words, I conjectured
that she did not get on well with the ladies of any
family ; and I fancy she had the evil fate, either
by intention or innocent inadvertence, to attract
a good deal too much of the notice of the husbands, brothers, sons, friends, and male visitors
generally, of the houses into which she was successively introduced.

I oftened marvelled that, in a place like London, so quick and clever a girl as Lilla could find
no way of converting her energy and ingenuity
into money. But practical capacity of this kind
she seemed not to have, or not to care about
exerting. I began to find, too, that the counsels

of her mother did not much tend to make her industrious to any purpose.

"My Lilly is a good girl," poor Mrs. Lyndon would say to me; "a good girl, Mr. Banks, although I say it. She ought to be a lady; and perhaps she will be one day. If I were dead and out of the way, I think, perhaps, they would make her a lady. She isn't fit to lead this kind of life; she's too delicate and too refined; anybody can see that. She can't eat the kind of dinners I have to set before her sometimes, poor child."

Lilla was immensely fond of the pastrycook's shop, and had a taste for lobster-salad as finely developed as ever I saw. There was something unspeakably touching in the manner and tone of the old woman when she spoke of this bouncing London lass, and the sincerity with which she evidently regarded her as too delicate and fragile for the coarse world around.

"She isn't strong like me," the emaciated old creature would say, the tears blinking in her sad and faded eyes. "I was a farmer's daughter, Mr. Banks, passing half my days in the fields and the open air, not like a poor peaky Londoner. I was a fine, stout, rosy girl at Lilly's age; and long

before that I could cook and bake and brew, and
put my hand to everything about the farm. Once
we had a great harvest-home dinner, and I cooked
a beautiful fawn for the day; and O, bless you,
the praise I got for it! My father called me up
to the table, and the farmers all drank my health,
and told me I'd make such a splendid farmer's
wife. I was that proud, I can tell you; and I
didn't expect then to be living in London a poor
old woman. But my poor Lilly was brought up
in town, and I never had much to give her, dear
child; and she can't be expected to look strong
and well as country girls do."

Mrs. Lyndon was not a widow. That piece
of information had been volunteered to me by
Lilla. Lilla told me her father had deserted them,
and gone abroad somewhere, and had not since
been heard of.

Sometimes when I came home late at night I
used to find my way down to the kitchen, where
the embers of the fire were generally burning, and
where I could smoke a pipe with a clear conscience,
having no curtains to fumigate and no one to render uncomfortable. One night, as I was going
down, I was surprised to see a light below. Think-

ing the gas had been left burning by mistake, I
went down; and when just on the last stair, I saw
that Mrs. Lyndon was still up. She was seated
with her back to me, and leant over the table.
Was she asleep? I stooped forward to see. No;
she was awake, and bent over something which
she was moving between her hands. Old stories
of misers in the depth of lonely night counting
their secret stores of gold, came whimsically
enough to my mind. She had no gold, however;
only a decayed old pack of blackened cards spread
before her. I softly withdrew; I had seen enough;
I had fathomed all the poor, sad little mystery
with one involuntary glance. I too was of Arcadia; I too had come up from the country, where
superstitions are still a faith, and omens and divi-
nations defy Hamlet's philosophy. I knew at once
that Mrs. Lyndon was trying some feeble, sad
sibylline work. Poor old creature, with her early
and childish country superstitions still clinging
round her, she was sorting the cards, to discover
in them some tidings of the husband who had
deserted her—some hint as to the fortunes of the
daughter whom she was breaking her heart to
bring up as a lady.

Late that night I heard a hansom cab drive
up to the door. I was reading something in my
own room, and I looked out of the window. Someone got out of the cab and handed Lilla to the
door-step. She was in opera costume—wherever
on earth she had got it—and she looked indeed
very attractive, and apparently very joyous, as she
tripped up the steps. It was an elderly gentleman
who accompanied her. I could see his iron-gray
hair and rather red face. Lilla opened the door
with her latch-key, while he got into the cab and
drove off. I could hear him giving directions to
the cabman in a peculiarly strident voice. Lilla
crept very softly downstairs, where I suppose her
mother was still sitting up for her.

Next morning I chanced to meet my young
friend. "O, Mr. Banks," she broke out, "I have
such a headache."

"You were dissipating last night," I answered.
"That is what comes of late hours."

"How do you know? Did you see me come
in?"

"Yes, that I did."

"I am so glad? Did I look well?"

"Charming."

"Did I really? Yes; my uncle took me to the Opera, and gave me the dress and cloak to go in —was not that kind of him?—and it was so delightful!"

"The music? What opera was it?"

"O, *Fidelio*. But I didn't care about the music; at least, I mean I didn't care so much about it. I was so happy, and delighted with everything, and especially myself. I was a lady for a whole night! And we were in the stalls— I love the stalls! I never was there before—and we had supper afterwards! And we drove home in a hansom. Now I have a headache; but I don't mind, for it's such a long time since I had a new dress; and I was so happy."

I could not help thinking of the poor old mother in the damp kitchen, spelling over her pack of cards.

Indeed I could never look at that poor old woman without wondering for what unknown purpose she was ever sent upon earth, in what inscrutable way Heaven would compensate her in some world hereafter for her joyless drudgery here. Not merely was she not happy herself, but with the kindliest heart, the most unselfish nature in the world, she did not seem to have the power of making anyone else happy. What hopeless misfortune had crushed her into beggarly inertness so young, I did not know ; but so long, at least, as Lilla's memory seemed to go back, the lives of the pair had been one unintermittent, humiliating, demoralising battle with poverty. Poverty and drudgery appeared to have crushed quite out of Mrs. Lyndon all the feeling of religion which everywhere but in London seems to cling to the old and the unfortunate. The butcher and baker left her no time to think of heaven. Her one thought was for her daughter : to get the pretty girl enough to eat, to cook tender chops for her, to have little dainties for her breakfast and her supper, to keep her in clothes, to guard her against consumption, to dream of her one day becoming a lady.

As for the daughter, she was simply a kind-hearted, bright, clever little heathen, not surely incapable of conversion and training if any high-minded creature could but take her in hand. Just now no Fayaway, no naked girl of South-Sea islands, could be a more thorough pagan than my graceful and pretty friend Lilla Lyndon.

CHAPTER IX.

MEANWHILE I am free to own that I liked the company of my pretty pagan; indeed, it brightened life very much to me. When I was most lonely and unfriended, these people had been strangely kind to me, and our common poverty and struggles made us—I was almost about to say unnaturally—certainly unusually familiar and friendly. Of course no young man of my age could ever be wholly indifferent to the company of a pretty and attractive girl; and I really grew quite fond of Lilla. I was not in the least in love with her, nor did she, I feel assured, ever think of me in the light of a possible lover; but we were very friendly and familiar, and indeed, in a sort of quiet confident way, attached to each other. A happy Bohemian independence of public opinion emancipated our movements. She

and I generally walked out together on Sundays
in the desolate suburbs, or across the swamp
which was undergoing slow conversion into a
park. Sometimes, as I came home in the evening, after giving some music-lessons — or, for
that matter, tuning a piano—I met her going
towards town, and I turned back and walked
with her. Much amazed I used to be at first
by her close knowledge of the shortest way to
get everywhere, and of every shop where the
best things to eat or wear or drink were to be
had at the lowest possible prices.

Our talk was generally lively enough ; but
there were days when I became so saddened by
my memories and my dull prospects that I
really could not brighten ; and then Lilla, in
order to encourage me, told me all kinds of
stories of her own occasional trials and dis-
tresses, as well as of people she had known,
who, having been reduced to the very depths of
despair, fell in with some lucky fortune, and
were raised at once to high position and afflu-
ence. Most of those stories, to be sure, were
told of young women reduced to serve in shops,
whom some men of enormous wealth fell in love

with and married; so that I could scarcely derive much encouragement from their application
to my own personal condition. But it was easy
to see with what a horizon fortune had bounded
poor Lilla's earthly ambition. She had no genius
for any work that did not directly conduce to
personal adornment, and she had a very strong
desire for wealth and ease.

"My only chance," she said frankly one
day, "is to marry somebody who has money.
I am sick of this place and this life. If I married a rich greengrocer even, I should be far,
far happier than I am. I should have a home
for my mother, and a cart to drive about in on
Sundays, when the greengrocer did not want it
for his business; and then mother and I would
leave him at home on the Sundays to smoke in
the back-kitchen, while we went out for a drive;
and we could call for you and take you with us.
I *must* marry somebody with money."

"Suppose, in the mean time, somebody without money comes in the way, and you fall in
love with him?"

"Love? Nonsense. Love is a luxury beyond my means, sir. Besides, do you know,

I think debts and poverty make some of us cold-hearted or no-hearted, and we are not capable of falling in love. Seriously, I don't think I could be."

"Then I hope no friend of mine will fall in love with you."

"I am sure I hope not—unless he has money. I don't believe I have such a thing as a heart."

"You ought to have told me all this before, Lilla. How do you know what agony you may be inflicting on my heart?"

I thought she would have laughed at this, but she looked at me quite gravely, and even sympathetically.

"Ah, no," she said quietly; "you are safe enough—from me at least; I can see that."

"Why, Miss Lyndon? Pray tell me."

"Don't ask me; but don't think me a fool. Have I not eyes? Can't I see that your heart is gone long ago in some disastrous way or other, and that you can't recover it; and don't you think I am sorry for you? Yes; as much as if you were my brother."

"Ah, Lilla, you have far more heart than

you would have me think. Not your eyes saw,
but your heart."

And we neither spoke any more on that subject. But I knew that under my pretty pagan's
plump bosom there beat a heart which the love
of lobster-salad, and the hopes of a rich husband,
and all the duty of dodging duns, could not
rob of its genial blood-warmth.

Lilla had, like most London girls of her class
and temperament, a passion for the theatre. She
knew the ways of every theatre, and something
about the private lives of all the actors and actresses, and who was married to whom, and who
were not married at all, and who was in debt,
and who made ever so much money in the year,
and spent it or hoarded it, as the case might be.
She pointed you out a small cigar-shop, and told
you it was kept by the father of Miss Vashner,
the great tragic actress; she called your attention to a small coal-and-potato store, and told
you it was there Mr. Wagstaffe, the great manager, began his career; she glanced at a beery,
snuffy little man in the street, and whispered
that he was the husband of the dashing Violet
Schönbein, who played the male parts in the

burlesques and pantomimes, and whose figure
was the admiration of London.   Her interest
did not lie so much in the stately opera-houses,
or even the theatres where legitimate tragedy
yet feebly protested its legitimacy and divine
right, as in the small pleasant houses where
comedians and piquant actresses could always
fill the benches. She knew where the best seats
were, and how to make use of an order to most
advantage ; and, indeed, seemed hardly ever to
have gone to a theatre except in the company of
somebody armed with such a missive. She had
been to parties of all kinds—to Kew, to Rich-
mond, to Vauxhall (yes, I think there was a
Vauxhall then), to Greenwich, to Dulwich, to
Rosherville. She appeared to have an intimate
knowledge of all the places where supper was to
be most comfortably and cheaply had in the
neighbourhood of each theatre. She had been
to the Derby; and she never missed seeing the
Queen going to open Parliament, or even the
Lord Mayor's Show. She knew all about the
great people of London—the Duchess of Suther-
land, Lady Palmerston, and the like ; and, by
some strange process of information, she often

used to get to know beforehand when grand balls
were given in the neighbourhood of Belgrave-
square or Park-lane, and she loved to go and
watch at the doors to see the ladies pass in.
Her uncle, she told me, had often promised to
take her to the Ladies' Gallery of the House of
Commons to hear a debate; but as yet he had
not carried out his promise. He took her to the
National Gallery and the Royal Academy's Exhi-
bition; but she did not much care about these
places of entertainment, and could not tell the
name of any picture or painter afterwards. Mr.
Lyndon, M.P., clearly wanted to impress her
with the necessity of some sort of mental culture, for he sent her a new piano and a heap
of books, and made her promise to learn. She
might have mastered most studies quickly enough
had she but shown the same aptitude for them
which she had for picking-up the private histories of actresses and great ladies, for turning
and trimming old dresses, for reviving decayed
bonnets, and for stimulating flat porter, by the
application of soda, into a ghastly likeness of
bottled stout.

I thought her naturally so clever, and indeed

I felt such a warm interest in her, that I set to work to teach her something. The piano she played very badly, and that I could teach her; singing I was likewise qualified to instruct her in; and French I spoke fluently enough. These, then, I offered, and in fact was determined, to teach her; and she was very glad to learn, and, when she was in humour for it, very quick and docile. What she went about teaching in the families where she had tried to be governess, I never could guess. Just now I was glad she knew so little, and that there were some things I could teach her. I had nothing to do half my time; I was lonely and unfriended; these people had been kind to me, as indeed kindness was a part of their nature, and I felt so grateful that I was only too glad to have any chance of showing my gratitude. So I became Lilla's music-master and French teacher when I could and when she would; and Mrs. Lyndon was delighted. The good woman trusted me entirely. She had so often told me what her dreams and hopes for her daughter were, that she knew so poor a caitiff as myself would never be mean enough to play Marplot by making love to Lilla. We were all poor together, and Mrs. Lyndon felt that hawks would not pick hawks' eyes out.

Little or nothing in this story turns upon my pupil-teaching of Lilla. In a direct sense, nothing came of it. I mention it here only to explain the fact that Lilla and her mother got to think themselves deeply indebted to me, and that Lilla in particular was determined to make me some return.

One evening I was walking rather listlessly along Sloane-street, feigning to myself that I had business in town, when I met Lilla returning homeward. She was all flushed and beaming, evidently under the influence of some piece of splendid good news.

"I have such news for you!" she said. "I have been to my uncle's, and I have talked to him about you."

"About me?"

"Yes. I always wanted to speak to him about you, and I made up my mind to go up specially to-day and do it. I told him all about you—how you were living in our house, and how kind you had always been to mamma and me—which I'm sure we don't forget—whenever we needed it; and Heaven knows we always do need it, for we never yet were able to pay anything at the right time."

"Well, well, pass over all that, and come back to Mr. Lyndon."

"Yes, I told him all about you, and how you were better than a colony of sons to mamma, and a whole schoolful of brothers to me, and how you teach me this and that—everything, in fact. I can tell you your ears ought to have tingled, for such praise as I gave you mortal man never yet deserved. I told him what a singer you were— ever so much better than Mario, I said; at which I promise you he smiled very grimly, and grumbled out that he had heard of too many singers who were ever so much better than Mario. But I told him that you were, and no mistake. And then I said you wanted to get on the stage, only that you had no friends; at which he smiled again, and said a man who could sing better than Mario didn't much stand in need of friends."

"Well, but, Lilla, I don't quite see."

"Don't you? No, I daresay you don't; but I just do. Why, did I never tell you that my uncle knows all the great swells about the theatres? O yes. He once had a share in a theatre with a tremendous swell, Lord Loreine, and he adores operas and singers, and he gives dinners at Greenwich to *prima donnas*. He is constantly behind the scenes everywhere—odd places for him to go to, I have often told him—and every great singer who comes out he always meets. Who is Reichstein? Is it a man or a woman?"

"Reichstein is a woman."

"Who is she?"

"A singer—a great success in Paris, I'm told. I don't know much about her—hardly anything, in fact. But she is new in Paris, and I believe a success."

"Well, he has been to Paris—indeed, he only came home last night—and he is in such a state about Reichstein, who is to come out in London and make a wonderful success. I was ashamed to confess that I never heard of Reichstein before, and didn't know, in fact, whether it was a man or a woman; and besides, I told him I wanted to talk about you, and not about Reichstein."

"What did he say?"

"He laughed and said, 'Reichstein could do more for your friend' (*my* friend, you understand)

'than I could.' In fact, he was in such a delightful good-humour, that I might have said anything
to him to-day. You are to come and see him.
O yes, you are; you'll find him very friendly."

"But, indeed, Lilla—"

"No, no; I can't hear any modest pleadings.
You are to come; I am to bring you. You may
be sure he'll like you; and, do you know, I really
begin to think your fortune is made. Perhaps
you may sing as *primo tenore* with what's-her-
name, Reichstein, some time. And I shall go to
hear you, and fling a bouquet to you—mind, not
to her—so be sure you keep it for yourself; and
then you must redeem your promise, and take me
to the Derby."

"Hear me swear! You shall accompany me
to the Derby. We'll have a carriage and, at least,
four horses the very first Derby-day after I have
sung as *primo tenore* with Mdlle. Reichstein."

"Well, you may laugh now; but I promise
you I'll make you keep your word. Far more un-
likely things have happened. But now tell me
when you are coming to see my uncle."

I had not the remotest idea of presenting myself or being presented to Lilla's uncle. All I

had heard of him pictured him to me as a cold, purse-proud, selfish, sensuous man—not, indeed, incapable of doing a generous thing for a poor dependent, but quite incapable of feeling any respect for poverty of any kind. His photograph, which Lilla often showed me, quite confirmed my notions of him. Egotism and pride were traced in every line of the face—of the straight square forehead, of the broad jaw—even the unmistakable sensuousness of the full lips and the wide mouth did not soften the general hardness of the expression. I cannot tell why, but I always detested the man. Patronage of any kind I must have hated ; but to be patronised by this rich man was utterly out of the question.

Yet I could not but feel grateful for the kindly manner in which poor Lilla had endeavoured to serve me. This was surely disinterestedness on her part. She so often had to solicit favours of her uncle upon her own account, that one might have imagined a shrewd and worldly girl would be very careful indeed not to weaken any influence she might have, not to discount any future concessions, by asking his good offices for another. Therefore, while I attached not the slightest importance to the promised influence, and would not have availed myself of it were it really to make my fortune in an hour, I took good care, the reader may well believe, to let Lilla see that I was not ungrateful. Nor did I dash her little pride and triumph by telling her that I would not go to see her uncle. But I temporised; and fortune gave me a ready way of doing it. I had been for some little time in negotiation about an engagement to join a company who were to give concerts in some of the provincial cities and towns; and this very day I had accepted the terms, and duly signed the conditions. I had therefore to leave town at once, and should probably be away for two or three months at the least.

This therefore gave me a satisfactory plea for postponing my visit to Mr. Lyndon.

Lilla was a little cast down; but as she knew I had long been anxious to secure this very engagement—my first of any note—she brightened up immediately, and gave me her warm congratulations.

"When I get back, Lilla, you shall make my fortune."

"How glad I shall be! Do you know that I

really hope you may not quite take the provinces by storm, and so find the way made clear to you, without my having anything to do with it? I do, indeed. I want so much to be the means of doing some good for you."

"You need not fear, Lilla. Fortune will be in no hurry to interfere with your kindly purpose."

"But stop. I *have* actually done something for you already. I have given you a name."

"Indeed! How is that?"

"Well, of course you can't call yourself Banks when you go on the stage. Banks would never do; there couldn't be a great Banks. Then you always say you never would consent to take any ridiculous Italian name."

"Never."

"Well, I have given you a delightful name, which is all your own, by the simplest process in the world. Temple Banks is absolutely ridiculous; people would always keep calling you Temple Bar. Now don't be angry."

"Indeed I am not."

"You got quite flushed when I laughed at your name, though; but no matter. Leave out the Banks altogether, and there you are—Emanuel

Temple! What can be prettier and softer? All liquids, positively. Well, I have made you Emanuel Temple, and nothing else. I spoke of you to my uncle as Emanuel Temple. He has written down your name in his memorandum-book as Emanuel Temple. I have launched you as Emanuel Temple, and Emanuel Temple you shall remain."

Nobody much likes any chaff about his name. I did not at first quite relish my young friend's remarks, but I soon saw there was some sense in them. I had indeed, for many reasons, determined on changing my name in some way, and this slight alteration would do as well as any other. So I went through the provinces as Emanuel Temple, and I have never since been publicly known by any other name.

CHAPTER X.

SOME few weeks of professional wandering among chilling audiences in country towns, meeting with tolerable success in most places, brought me to Dover, and the first glimpse of the sea I had enjoyed for years. I felt boyish again at the sight of my old confidant; and the shining track of the moon across the water seemed to mark out a bright path back to the delightful dreamland, the far-off, fading Island of the Blest, with its "light of ineffable faces," whither my boyhood and my first love were banished, the one seemingly as much lost to me as the other. Not for years had I thought so bitterly, so passionately, of Christina as during my short stay in Dover by the sea. And yet she seemed to me almost like a creature in a dream—like some beautiful spirit-love, which had descended upon me while I lay in ecstatic delirium, and faded with my waking. I can al-

most believe the stories of men who have fallen
madly in love with the daughters of dreams, and
pined and sickened away their lives in longing
after the unreal, and were glad to die, that they
might be relieved of the vain tormenting wish.

I pass, however, from recalling these purely
personal and egotistical recollections to the subject
which I meant to speak of when I recurred to my
visit to Dover. An accidental meeting there threw
me in the way of making an odd acquaintanceship,
which had no little influence afterwards on one
part at least of my fortunes, and those of two distinct and divided sets of persons, whose histories
make indirectly a chapter of mine.

One evening, after I had sung at a concert
and been somewhat applauded, I went to have
my customary stroll by the sea. I turned into
a cigar-shop in one of the steep, stony, narrow
little streets, chiefly made up of oyster-shops and
public-houses, which alone are astir in Dover after
nightfall. I asked for a cigar, hardly observing
that somebody else was being served with something by the young woman who stood behind the
counter.

" Glad *he's* come in !" said a full mellow male

voice; "very glad. *He'll* decide; he looks a sort
of person who ought to know."

It did not occur to me that this could well have
any reference to myself, and so I asked again for
a cigar. I noticed then that the girl was flushed
in the face, and was biting her lips, half amused
and half angry.

"Shall I refer it to him?" said the male voice
again.

"I really don't care," replied the girl, "whom
you refer it to; I've told you the price and the
quality, that's all."

I looked round, and saw that there was seated
on a chair at my left a short, stout, well-preserved
elderly personage, with black, beady, twinkling
eyes, shining white teeth, a rubicund complexion,
and a black wig. His opened lips had a full, sensuous expression, and there was a dash of something
in his whole face which vaguely spoke of cruelty,
or marked eccentricity, or something else that is
out of the commonplace character of the every-day
Briton. There was an odd, indefinable mixture
about his appearance and manner of the broken-
down gentleman and the artist. I should say
that he was probably a naturalised Bohemian,—

one not born among the gipsies, but who perhaps
had strayed into their encampments in early life,
or got changed at nurse. His uncommon appearance and queer ways struck me at once. I observed that his hands were small, fat, and beauti-
fully white.

"Then we refer the case to arbitration," complacently remarked this personage; and, still remaining in his chair, he touched his hat very
graciously to me, and with a wave of his hand
invited my attention. "We have had a dispute,
sir, I and this young lady—her name is Fanny; I
address her by her name because we are old
acquaintances; I have been here twice, I think—
touching the quality of these cigars. She declares
them to be prime Havanas, and has the conscience
to ask eightpence each. *I* represent them to be
rather inferior Veveys, and suggest one penny
each, or seven for sixpence. On these terms I
am willing to treat for one shilling's worth. I
tell her frankly it is no use trying to deceive
me. I have been to Havana, and I have only just
come back from Switzerland; and I remark to her
that I rather think I saw the light at least a year
or two before she did, and that, generally speak-

ing, I have not knocked about the world for nothing. She refuses to admit the force of these arguments. Fortunately you have come in just in time to arbitrate. You seem to me a man who ought to know tobacco from dock-leaves and brown paper. Come, then, how say you—Havana or Vevey?"

"I am afraid I must decline to arbitrate. I have not been to Havana."

" But you are not a Dover man ? You don't belong to this confounded dirty, disgraceful little place? Don't tell me."

" No, I am not a Dover man."

" Of course not ; I knew it.—You see, Fanny, it's no use trying to deceive me. Take example, sweet girl."

The sweet girl only tossed her head and looked remarkably sour.

" If you're not going to 'ave the cigars," she said, "I just wish you'd put them down, and not bother."

" Fanny, you rush to conclusions with the impetuosity of your sex. It must be something, I fancy, in the nature of petticoats that makes the wearers of them so quick in their conclusions.

No, Fanny, I shall not put the cigars down, because I do mean to ''ave them,' as you express it, with the delicious disregard of aspirates peculiar to our common country. I mean to ''ave them' and to pay for them, fair being, even at your own price; but I am anxious to convince you that, though you may extort my money—"

"Extort, indeed! I don't care, I'm sure, if you 'ave them or don't 'ave them."

"''Ave them or don't 'ave them.' Innocent accents! As I was observing when I was interrupted—pray don't go, sir, one moment—I want to convince you that you cannot cheat me, or confound my sense of justice. You may fret me, but you cannot play upon me. I am only for justice. All my life through I have stood up for justice, and I never could get it. The whole world and his wife were against me, may God curse them all!—Look here, sir!" And he jumped off his seat, and came close up to me, throwing his hat back off his forehead as he did so, and much disarranging his wig meantime. "Have you ever been conspired against, and hated?"

"No, I think not; I don't know at least; and pardon me if I say I don't much care."

"And do you think *I* care? Not I. They have done their best for years, and I have stood out against them, and defied them, and bade them go to the devil; and just because they wouldn't go, and wanted me very particularly not to go either, I did my utmost to go there as fast as possible."

"Which I do believe you're going," muttered the girl, with a glance at me.

"I am a victim, sir, to my sense of justice, and my determination not to be conquered. I left England when they wanted me to stay here; I come back now because I know they want me away. I'll spoil their game. There are people would rather see all the Beelzebubs and Molochs and Asmodeuses, and the rest of them, than me. Therefore I come. ' Confound their politics ; frustrate their knavish tricks !' Good-evening, sir. Or, stay, are you walking my way, and will you permit me to walk a little with you ?"

I was about to decline very firmly the proffered companionship, but a supplicating look from poor Fanny seemed to beg of me to take him out of her way, wheresoever he might then desire to go. So I was pleased to be able to oblige the perplexed lass, who seemed half talked to death already; and it really did not much matter to me whether I endured my new acquaintance's company for a few minutes longer or got rid of him at once. So I expressed myself as quite delighted to have the pleasure of his company, and I was thanked by a glance of gratitude from under Fanny's eyelids.

"Good-night, then, Fanny. Farewell, a long farewell, my Fanny; perchance I may revisit thee no more. I take these six—Havanas we'll call them—at your own valuation. This gentleman and I are too much pressed for time to enter on the business of an arbitration now; and besides, I don't think I could trust him—for he is young, Fanny, and inexperienced—to arbitrate between me and so pretty a girl as yourself. Between man and man is easy arbitration, Fanny; but between man and woman is trying work. Six cigars at eightpence each : six times eight, forty-eight— four shillings. The roof does not fall in, Fanny! I perceive that the Powers above have no intention of interfering to punish or prevent fraud; and I have only to pay. There are the four shillings. Farewell, Fanny; repent, and remember me!—Now, then, sir, at your service."

I followed my whimsical acquaintance. I observed that all his clothes were of foreign cut and fashion, and looked rather decaying. Indeed, he might have been taken for a shabby old Frenchman who had once been in good society, but for his voice and accent. These were unmistakably English. His voice was peculiarly sweet, full, and mellow, and its natural intonation when he dropped the manner of roystering buffoonery, which seemed to me purposely put on, was decidedly that of an educated English gentleman.

"That's a pretty little devil," remarked my friend as we emerged from a dark street suddenly into the moonlight of the quay.

"The girl in the shop?"

"As if you didn't know at once whom I meant! Of course the girl in the shop—I daresay you'll be found dropping in upon her again."

"Not likely at all."

"Lord, Lord, how this world is given to lying! Don't be offended, sir; I have only been quoting Jack Falstaff."

"I know, and I am not offended."

"Thanks; I begin to think you are rather a good sort of fellow in your way, and I only offend people I don't like. But you know very well, you sly rogue, you'll be looking in on little Fanny again. I saw telegraphic glances passing between you."

" I don't care one rush ever to see her again, and I don't mean to."

" How odd! They tell me young fellows in England are greatly changed since my time. Apparently so. When I was your age, I should have liked to see such a girl more than once. Even now, I can assure you, I am a martyr, a positive martyr, to my general affection for the petticoat. But look there! God! how can a man talk of petticoats, and such fribbles and *frou-frou*, when he has a sight like that before him ?"

He pointed to the sea. We had reached a part of the road from which you looked, on the one hand, at the grand old castle and the white cliffs; on the other, out across the waves, whereon the soft moonlight of late summer seemed floating. The muffled, gentle thunder of the waters rolling languidly and heavily on the strand was in our ears; the scent of the salt sea in our nostrils; the summer air all around us; the moon and the

sea before our eyes. It was indeed a scene to re-
fine even vulgarity, to solemnise frivolity.

My friend took off his hat, and stood gazing on
the sea. Presently I heard him murmur in his
deep soft tones: "For I have loved, O Lord,
the beauty of thy house, and the place where thine
honour dwelleth." He presently turned to me:
"Do you think it will avail a man hereafter to
plead that he has loved the beauty of His house?"

"Surely, surely; at least I hope so.

"Then you are an artist." This was said in
the tone of one who has suddenly made a gratify-
ing discovery.

"Well, a sort of artist; at least not wholly
without some kind of artistic taste."

"You believe in beauty, don't you? Now,
don't give me any vague commonplace answer—I
hate cant and parroting of any kind. If you don't
believe in it, or if you don't quite know what I
mean when I ask you the question, then say you
don't, and let there be an end of it. A man may
be a devilish good fellow although he has no more
soul for beauty than that rock yonder; and let me
tell you a man may be a devilish bad fellow, and
guilty of pretty well every sin that ever came in

his way, although he is open at every pore to the contagion of beauty wherever it shows itself, in a wave or a moonbeam or a woman's bosom. The thing is, do you believe in beauty? Because, if not, we had better walk on, and talk about oysters and cigars."

I never was fluent with confessions of faith on the spur of the moment; and I was not quite clear about the perfect sanity of my companion. However, I answered quite truly that I thought I might describe myself as, in his sense, a believer in beauty.

"Good—we are companions. Now, then, let us look at that scene for a little, and, like a good fellow, don't keep talking all the while." (I had not uttered six sentences thus far during our walk.) "Such a sight must be enjoyed in silence. It is holy; yes, damn me, but it is."

After this pious affirmation he relapsed into silence—only, however, for a few minutes.

"I have been an artist," he said; "at least I tried to paint pictures. I think they were very good, but they didn't come to anything. In fact, with me nothing comes to anything. I was brought up to be a gentleman, and that didn't

prosper much with me. I've been a ballad-singer
—fact! give you my word on it. I've sung in
London squares, outside the windows of houses
where I've many a time dined; and they've sent
out the confounded flunkey to tell me to move on.
True, every word of it!" And he burst into a loud
peal of laughter, which waked the echoes of the
cliffs, and sounded like a startling hideous profanity of the stillness and the scene.

"The singing did not prosper ?" I asked calmly,
not out of any particular curiosity, but to interpose any question which might check his disso-
nant mirth.

"Not it! Nothing, I have told you already,
ever does prosper with me; and yet they can't get
rid of me, I can tell you."

" *They* ?"

"Yes, they. What is it to you who they are,
or what their accursed names are ? "

"I assure you I don't want to know at all."

" They? I'll tell you who *they* are. The phari-
sees, the publicans, the respectable hypocrites,
the cold, confounded, bloodless, sinless devils.
Look here, and answer me truly—did you ever do
a virtuous action ?"

"Really, that depends—"

"No, it doesn't; it depends on nothing. Did you ever do anything that was really virtuous and self-denying, that you would much rather not have done, but did because virtuous people asked you to do it? Anything of that sort have you ever done?"

"Well, if you press me for an answer, I must say I don't believe I ever did."

"Of course you never did. Well, I did once! You'll not catch me doing such a thing again, I can tell you; it played the devil with me. I've done—and I had done before that—about every foolish and bad thing a man could do; but I might have been forgiven everything except the one sacrifice to virtue. And it was *such* a sacrifice! If you only knew! No matter. Are you leaving Dover soon?"

"In a day or two."

"Going over, no doubt?"

He nodded in the direction where the French coast lay, now of course wholly lost to sight.

"No. I am going to visit a few towns here in the south."

"And then?"

"Then to London."

"Where you live?"

"Where I live."

"Good. I am going to live there too—unless I happen to starve there—for a while. I have a few coins left. I should think a week of very rigid economy would play them out, and Heaven knows into what company of thieves I may fall meantime."

Something prompted me to say with more emphasis than if the words were merely formal, "I hope we may meet in London."

He laughed a short laugh.

"Well," he said, "*I* hope so too; but if, as the final result of our meeting, you are particularly glad of the acquaintance, I think you'll be about the first that ever had occasion to express such a sentiment. And yet I love mankind; and I really don't try to do harm to anybody, except to some very, very near and dear relatives. I suppose London stands where it did, and is much the same as usual?"

"Just as it was so long as I can remember it."

"I thought so. All the young men wise, and

all the young women virtuous. All the marriages made in heaven, and all husbands devoted to their wives. All brothers of course living together in love and harmony. A blessed place! Naturally just the place for me: so I am going there. I have not been there for years; but I am glad to hear that its beatific condition remains still unaltered."

He snapped his fingers, and turned abruptly away from me. Just as I thought I had got rid of him, however, he wheeled round and came sharply up to me again.

"Do you know anybody in London?" he asked.

"Very few people. In your sense I should perhaps say nobody."

"Any members of parliament, for example?"

"Not one."

"Ah, that's a pity! Some of them are such noble fellows; *I* know some of them. I know one in particular, and I am very fond of him. His name is Tommy Goodboy. An odd name, isn't it? But it's his name. Don't look in Dod when you get home for Tommy Goodboy, Esq. M.P., because he doesn't give his real name when

he goes to the House of Commons. But he's
Tommy Goodboy. You remember the story of
Tommy and Harry? Harry didn't care; and so
a roaring lion came and ate him up. That was
convenient for the good people, the respectable
and well-behaved people. The deuce of the thing
would have been if Harry didn't get eaten, but
came back all alive, and kept tormenting Tommy
out of his wretched, pitiful existence, disgracing
him, crouching at his door like Lazarus, and
offending the guests whom Tommy invited to
dinner.—By the way, I take it for granted you
are hard up?"

"Well, I certainly am not Dives. No beggar
would care to wait at my door."

"No, I thought not. You dress well enough;
but there is something unmistakable about the
cut of the man who is hard up. 'Poor devil' is
written in every line of *you;* and yet I should
say you are a sort of fellow who will burst out
of all that and get on. Unlike me in that respect; *I* am a poor devil, and I never shall get
on. Good-night. I daresay we shall meet again
somewhere. I am going back to the town. I
know a very pleasant place where oysters are

eaten, and brandy is drunk, and songs are sung;
and I am a sort of king of the feast there. They
are all low scoundrels, and I'm a kind of lord and
patron among them. I don't suppose it's any use
asking *you* to come."

" Thanks, no; not the slightest."

" No, you don't seem just the sort of person
to enliven a convivial gathering. I know what's
the matter with you. Don't be cast down, man;
you and she will meet again yet."

His idle words did, I suppose, make me give
a slight start; for he laughed his chuckling rolling laugh, and said:

" So I have touched you! I thought as much.
Confound it, man! you're as fortunate as one of
Virgil's rustics, if you only knew your own good
luck. The best thing that can happen to you is
never to see her again; and to keep up your
poetry, and romance, and despair, and all the
rest of the nonsense. Take my word for it, if
you have the misfortune to marry her, you'll soon
find the poetry and the romance sponged out, and
you'll be glad to join me at the oysters and the
brandy! Despairing lover, I envy you from my
soul! By God, I do! I would give the crown of

England, if I had it, to be young like you, and
to be disappointed in love. It's glorious! Confound it, you've made me so envious that I'll
leave you with a parting malediction. May the
devil inspire her to marry you!"

He burst into his laugh again, and trotted
away at last townwards. I was glad to get rid
of him; indeed, for the last few minutes of the
conversation, I was plagued by a strong desire to
kick him—a performance hardly practicable, seeing that he was old enough to be my father, and
only half my size. Yet it was strange with what
interest I had been studying his face, his voice,
his gestures, all the time that he was speaking.
I felt perfectly satisfied that I had never seen him
before, and yet there was something tormentingly,
tantalisingly familiar to me in his features. It
was some shadowy, quick-darting resemblance
which every now and then seemed just on the
point of revealing itself, but always vanished at
the most critical moment. As one tortures himself in trying to recall a name which is every
instant on the tip of the tongue and yet will not
come out, so I perplexed myself in vain endea-
vours to read the riddle of his face and voice.

Strangely too, it seemed to remind me, as well as I could understand my own sensations, not of one, but of two faces I had somewhere seen. The upper part of the face, the bright twinkling eyes, the straight short nose, the cheekbones just a little high, the white forehead,—these were features which reminded me of something that brought with it genial and kindly associations; while the sensuous lips and cruel jaw recalled something which was harsh and displeasing to remember. I racked my brain again and again; and indeed I think that I dreamed of the creature half through the night, and thought I saw him turning before my eyes into the successive resemblances of nearly every man I knew. But I awoke in the morning with the riddle still unexplained, and at last I resolutely put it aside altogether.

CHAPTER XI.

THAT night we gave another concert; it was well attended, and successful. When I came on to take part in a duet with some woman, I naturally looked round the hall, and to my mingled amusement and vexation I saw my friend of the previous night seated in the reserved part of the hall, and listening with his head a little to one side, and all the manner of a professed connoisseur. He beat time gently with his fingers; he nodded his head and smiled a sweet approving smile when some passage was specially well executed; his brows contracted and he shook his head in indignant remonstrance at anything out of time or tune. To do him justice, he really did seem to know something about the music, which hardly anybody else among the audience did. Therefore he took quite a leading part in the reserved seats, looked blandly but command-

ingly around, and intimated with eye or gesture where applause might properly be awarded;
frowned fiercely down any untimely burst coming
in at a wrong place; shrugged his shoulders and
shuddered when a breath of wholly unmerited approval floated past him; cried *bravo* to a singer,
brava to a songstress, *bravi* when more than one
performer conquered his approval; expressed in
audible tones his final verdict on each performance; and, in short, conducted himself quite as
one whose judgment artists and audience had
alike agreed to recognise. Whether he remembered me or not, I could not guess, for his face
gave no token of recognition. But when I came
on, I observed that he took, with an air of
gracious friendliness, the programme from the
lap of a lady who sat next him, and raising a
double-eyeglass which he wore, looked down the
bill apparently to discover my name. He was
very patronising in his treatment of me; only
shrugged his shoulders once or twice, and several
times tapped his palms together and cried " bravo!" Indeed, I think he encouraged, at all events
he permitted, an *encore* of one of my ballads. He
showed to most advantage, however, during the

second part of the concert, which was made up of selections from an oratorio. Impressed strongly by his manner, and apparently anxious to do some act of homage to so accomplished a critic, the lady next him offered to allow him to read from the score of the oratorio she had with her. His manner of surprised, amused, pitying, condescending rejection of the proffered kindness was sublime. The shrug of the shoulders, the raising of the eyebrows, the graceful, lordly waving of the disclaiming hand, the bend of the head, the benign, superior smile, all said as plainly as words could have spoken it : "My dear madame, do you really suppose there is one note, one half-note of this music that is not familiar to me as the letters of the alphabet? A thousand thanks for your well-meant offer ; but pardon me if I say that it really *does* amuse me."

When I was leaving the hall at the end of the performance I caught another glimpse of my friend. He was making himself painfully attentive to two ladies, perhaps those who had sat next to him, by insisting on opening their carriage-door for them, handing them in, arranging their skirts, and otherwise playing the gallant, much to

their apparent vexation. He then shut the carriage-door, took off his hat and bowed profoundly,
and in a loud tone gave the coachman his order
for "home." I watched him for a while with
considerable amusement. He then stood on the
pavement and scrutinised the crowd coming out.
A lady and gentleman came out, talking together
in French. The sound struck my friend's ears;
he at once approached them, took off his hat,
made a bow, and addressed them in a voluble
stream of French, accompanying his words with
such gestures and shrugs and elevation of eye-
brows, that he seemed to have transformed himself into a very Frenchman all in a moment. I
do not know whether he was really passing himself off as a Frenchman, but the persons he
addressed stopped and conversed with him for a
moment or two, then seemed to be puzzled by
him, then evidently became anxious to shake him
off, finally nodded a good-humoured, peremptory
adieu, and literally broke away from him. Whereupon my friend first stamped on the pavement,
muttered something about *canaille*, then swore a
round Saxon oath or two, then burst into a loud
laugh, and went laughing and stamping down the

street. I passed him quite closely. He did not observe me ; at least he took no notice whatever of me. He was talking to himself.

" The society of the just declines to have me this night," I heard him say. " I have given it the chance, once, twice. The stuck-up Britoness scorns my attentions, confound her ! I wish she was Boadicea, and I one of the Roman conquerors, furnished with a good birchen rod. Neither will the frog-eating, fantastic fribble of France invite me to sup with himself and his wife. Afraid to run such a risk with her, no doubt. I don't wonder. I can't sit at good men's feasts to-night. No help for it. There are worse things than bad men's feasts, that's one comfort."

I did not care to give him the chance of fastening on me, whether he chose to regard me as of the good or of the bad ; so I hurried away, and so far I escaped.

I walked and smoked a good deal by the seaside that night, and enjoyed the solitude and the beauty of the place. In a very few days I was to return to London, after an absence that had now spread over some months—my first absence, even for a week, since I had come to live in the great

city. I thought of Lilla and her good-natured
undertaking to make my fortune through her
uncle's influence, and wondered how I should be
able to get rid of the offer without wounding her,
or seeming ungrateful for her kindness. If I
could only spread out my provincial engagement
for even a fortnight or three weeks longer, the
season would be over by the time I had returned
to town, and Mr. Lyndon would probably have be-
taken himself to Ems, or Baden, or Florence, and
the difficulty would be obviated for another season
at least.

I could not think of such things without medi-
tating rather sadly over my own dreary life and
blank future, and then falling into the old, old
track of thought about my lost Christina, who
had so literally disappeared out of my life.
Strange, that in wandering about London I had
never met even Ned Lambert, our quondam bass-
singer; who might perhaps have told me something of her—whose face would at least have recalled more vividly the associations of the dear,
fading days of long ago. Poor Ned Lambert!
he must have suffered much. But, good heavens,
what could his sufferings have been to mine! He

at least was not first raised up to happiness, and then flung down to despair; while I—O heaven, how happy I was once!

Of late I found myself growing quite moody and moping. I began to think I was getting prematurely old, and to look out of mornings for gray hairs—at eight-and-twenty!

I turned away from the seashore, and walked homeward through the town. Passing through one of the streets, I heard noise, clamour, shouting, cursing, stamping—apparently going on in a low public-house, the light from whose windows was the only bright spot along that side of the street. As I came up to the place, its swing-doors were suddenly flung open, and the "row" streamed out upon the pavement. It assumed the form of a little crowd of men hustling and rushing round some central figures. There were shouts of "Give it him!" "Let 'im 'ave it!" "No!" "Shame!" "Don't hit him!" "Knock him down!" "Damnation Frenchman!" "Dirty foreigner!" "Call the police!" and so forth. I could see that the fat, bare-headed landlord, and the almost equally fat barman, were wildly endeavouring to restore order, or keep the whole company out, while the barmaid stood at the door and vainly screamed for the "Perlice!"

I do not feel much interest in "rows," and would gladly have passed on, but the "row" broke around me, so to speak, split into waves upon the sudden and unexpected opposition of my advancing form, and I found myself somehow in the very midst of it. Then I saw that the central figures were a big, stout, lubberly-looking cavalry soldier, and a small man, who was clinging to the hero's neck. In the latter figure I at once recognised my fantastic friend of the black wig. He was jabbering away in a jargon of French and broken English, and was clinging to his antagonist like a savage little bulldog. Just as I was rushing in to endeavour to get him away, the big soldier succeeded in shaking himself free from my friend's grip, and then took the little man bodily off his feet, and flung him on the pavement, amid a yelling chorus of cheers and laughter, broken by a few cries of "Shame!"

"For shame, you cowardly ruffian!" I exclaimed, utterly ignorant as I was of the merits of the quarrel. "Don't you see he is an old man! Fight your match, you blackguard, if you want to fight f"

I fully expected to have had to accept a practical challenge on my own account, and stood therefore quite ready, the first moment the soldier made an attack on me, to hit hard and home. He was a floundering, awkward sort of fellow. I was stout and sinewy at that time, and had some little science. I did not despair of finishing-off the battle in a well-employed minute or so.

But to do the honest warrior justice, he seemed rather ashamed of his part in the transaction.

"Who wants to fight him?" he asked in a growling tone, and with a sheepish expression. "He ain't that old, neither; but I didn't want to have anything to do with the dirty little Frenchy. 'Twas all his work. Why didn't he let me alone? Why did he keep badgerin' of me, and worryin' of me, and insultin' of me and my red coat, all the evening?"

There was a chorus of approbation, and the barman cried "Hear, hear!"

Meanwhile my little friend jumped to his feet again, and began to dance around us on the pavement without hat or wig, presenting so outrage-

ously ridiculous a spectacle, that I could not
wonder at the roar of laughter with which he was
greeted. I kept between him and the soldier as
well as I could, and I at last seized him fast
round the arms, while he, endeavouring to break
away and get at his antagonist, dragged and
whirled me round on the pavement in a manner
the most grotesque and ludicrous.

"Let him come!" roared the absurd little
beast, in his ridiculous jabber. "*Cochon d'un
Anglais!* God dam John Bull! Poltroon of
militaire! I am not so old, *moi*, but I can
teach *ce gros militaire* his own *boxe*. Coward
English! English dam! Fight you all round!
Sacré-é-é-é!"

The absurdity and whimsicality of the whole
scene, and of this ridiculous little being's nonsen-
sical part in it, were altogether too much for me,
and I too joined in the burst of laughter.

"Come, come," I said at last, shaking my old
friend rather roughly by the collar, "don't make
a fool of yourself any more. You have had
enough of this for one night. Come away with
me."

"Will ze *gros militaire* make apology?"

A renewed burst of laughter followed this, in which the *gros militaire* himself joined.

"Do take him away, like a good gentleman," said the landlord to me. "I do think he's the most worriting little creature as ever I saw. He's been insulting everyone in my bar to-night. He kissed my barmaid, and he wanted to kiss my wife; and he's been so down upon that there soldier as flesh and blood wouldn't stand it, telling him the English soldiers were all cowards, and that the French were coming over to thrash us all and carry off our wives. And I tried to get rid of him quietly, and he wouldn't go, and I tried to keep order; but you know it's hard for Englishmen to stand being insulted by a d—d little Frenchman; and the soldier didn't hit him at all, but only wanted just to put him out of the place."

"Well, take all these people in again, and I'll get him out of this.—No, you sha'n't." This last assurance was given to my impetuous friend, who was plunging and struggling so, that it sometimes took all the vigour of my eight-and-twenty years to keep him back, and indeed I sometimes felt tempted to let him rush on and get smothered or

set-upon by the cavalry-man. The crowd, however, seeing that the fun was probably over, began
to straggle back laughing into the public-house;
the barman and the barmaid had returned to their
duties; the soldier was only too glad to get out of
the whole business; and I was nearly master of
the situation.

"Here's his hat," said the landlord.

"And here's his wig!" exclaimed a bystander,
with a burst of laughter.

The soldier having by this time disappeared
behind the swing-doors of the public-house, his
antagonist allowed himself to be quietly *coiffé*;
and having shrugged his shoulders several times,
and exclaimed that the *chasseur* acknowledged
himself *vaincu*, he made a low bow to the few
remaining spectators, thanked *ces braves Anglais*
for the fair-play of the *boxe*, and, leaning on my
arm affectionately, consented to be led away. The
disgust I felt at the whole business no words can
express. But that I looked at his withered face,
and saw the deepening ruts of Time's track so
plainly in it, I should have regretted that I had
not left the soldier and himself to settle the business between them.

When we had got a few paces from the scene
of conflict, my companion burst into a long peal
of rolling laughter.

" That was capital," he chuckled. " Did you
ever see such fun ? I suppose I may drop the
Frenchman now, and return to my allegiance as a
native-born subject of happy and glorious, long to
reign over us, Victoria, Queen of Great Britain
and Ireland."

" What on earth led you to carry on all that
absurd buffoonery ?"

"If I know, may I be condemned to the eter-
nal society of British respectability ! Give you
my word, my dear young friend—whose name I
have not yet the honour of knowing—I can no
more tell you why I chose to assume the manners, prejudices, and lingo of Albion's hereditary
enemy than I could solve the mystery of man's
hereafter. What then ? We are all creatures of
impulse. I have been especially so from the date
of my first misfortune—of course, I mean my
birth. I looked into that atrocious den there with
no object whatever. I might have come harm-
lessly away in five minutes, when the evil destinies would have it that my wandering eyes fell

upon that hapless soldier. He was the centre of
an admiring bumpkin or costermonger group; he
was telling, I think, his adventures—atrocious
lies, of course, every one—in China, or the Khy-
ber Pass, or Syria, or some other place; and he
was evidently immensely proud of being a British
soldier. May I perish if I could resist the temptation to make him and the rest of them uncomfortable! The one thing I hate in life is smug
and sleek respectability and self-conceit, in any
sphere whatever. In that moment I became a
Frenchman—positively for the time being I was a
Frenchman. I soon disturbed the harmony of
the festive hour. I confuted my red-coat with
impromptu facts and impossible geography. I
bewildered him so far that before long he couldn't
have told whether he did or did not take part in
the battle of Plassy, and whether Marshal Ney did
not lick the English there. I contradicted and
chaffed him, every word he said; I kissed the
barmaid because he seemed spoony about her; I
winked ostentatiously at the landlord's wife, until
mine host grew purple with jealousy and fear—I
really believe I kissed her too; and finally—"

"Finally, they kicked you out."

"No, they didn't. The soldier tried to put me out, and couldn't, and then the whole of them fell on me somehow; and I have no doubt they would all have wreaked their base vengeance on me but that you came gallantly up to the rescue. I owe you something for that. So much the worse for you. The people I owe anything to are seldom any the better for it. Yet I like you; I did from the first. You look so confoundedly out of sorts."

"Thank you."

"Yes, you do. I hate success and respectability. I hate virtue, and domestic happiness, and the proprieties, and all that revolting stuff. I detest children and wives, and people who parade their chubby, insolent happiness. Stand there—just there—in the moonlight a little, and let me look at you."

I complied with his wish. He planted me as a painter might his model, fell back to a proper distance, and steadily surveyed me with his piercing, glittering, small black eyes.

"Yes, that will do," he said reflectively. "Nothing about you to offend me. You don't seem to me to have tasted much success in life,

or to be particularly happy. You, I should say,
are at odds with the world, and likely to be for a
time at least, and then, perhaps, you may come
out all right; and if you do, I don't want to see
any more of you from that time forth. Did you
ever hear of Swift and his *sæva indignatio*, which
could only leave him with his life?"

"Yes, I *have* heard of Swift, and know all
about his *sæva indignatio*."

"Well, I think that's my curse. I writhe
under it, and I live to make others writhe. That
one resemblance—you need not tell me it is the
only one—I bear to Jonathan Swift. How the
devil, though, do you know it is the only one?"

"I didn't say I knew anything about it. You
may be twice as great a man as Swift for aught
I know to the contrary."

"Of course I may—to be sure I may. Then
why did you sneer when I spoke of a resemblance
between Swift and myself?"

"I didn't sneer. I smiled at the notion."

"Don't smile any more until you know what
you are smiling at. However, I don't mind being
frank and humble for once, and confessing that
in the matter of genius I am decidedly inferior

to Swift. Also that the world has never recognised me as it did him. But one thing is certain: Swift never locked up in his heart a greater treasure of hate than I do. How old are you?"

"Twenty-eight, I think, or thereabouts."

"Don't you find the world a devilish place?"

"How devilish?"

"Full of devils. Here, there, and everywhere —devils all around us. If I were inclined to be an atheist—which, thank God, I never, never was —I should be forced to believe in God, because I see so much of the devil. Don't you think with me?"

"O yes, quite so; no doubt. In fact, I am rather in a hurry now, and can't stay to discuss theology."

"Another sneer! This time an inexcusable one, for it is a sneer against religion. Young man, whatever you do, be religious always."

I was turning away, utterly disgusted at the hideous profanation of his language. He saw disgust painted on my features, and he seized me by the arm:

"Stay; don't go yet. Don't—you sha'n't. You think me a hypocrite?"

"I do; and I am sickened by such talk. Let me go, and good-night."

"No; just listen to me. I am not a hypocrite; no, by God! *He* hears me, and He knows! If I had been, I must have succeeded in life, and been respectable, and had carriages and fine horses, and sat in Parliament as Tommy Goodboy. But I could not; I would go my own way —to the devil if need be—and yet loving religion all the time. What else is my hope and my consolation? Do I not read in the Psalms of David how he curses his enemies?—and these words teach *me* how to curse mine. Do I not read how Dives at last went down to hell—"

"For shame, for shame! You are growing old, and should read the Holy Scriptures to some other purpose, or not at all. Let us say no more of it—and good-night."

"Good-night, then—and go to the devil! I say, shall we meet in London?"

"I hope not."

"Then I hope we shall; and I am sure we shall; I see it in the future that we are to be thrown together a good deal somehow."

Confound it! this very thought was at the

moment pressing painfully on my own mind. Just as I still kept thinking his face not unfamiliar to me, and wondering where I could have seen one like it before, so I began now to be weighed down with a hideous foreboding that this creature and I were likely to be brought together in some close and disagreeable way hereafter. The very nourishing of this thought drew with it a hesitation which unconsciously checked my abrupt breaking away from my companion. Involuntarily, irresistibly, I once more set myself to scan and study his features, in the vague hope of reading there some clue to my forebodings.

"I see you don't like the prospect," he remarked with a chuckle; "but *you* need not much fear: you have no money, I know. Lucky for you, for I must get money somehow; and I am *such* a hand at billiards and cards! But I can't wait for these slow and steady acquisitions when I get to London. I must have something to open the campaign with. *Gare* to Goodboy! Goodbye to you for the present; we'll meet again. Just now take your face hence. Thanks for defending me so valiantly. Next time that, in the capacity of a discharged *caporal*, I am engaged in vindicating the honour of France against some gigantic beef-eating Briton, I'll endeavour to have *you* close at hand."

At last he went away; and I could hear him trolling *Partant pour la Syrie* in a wonderfully sweet and mellow voice as he disappeared from my sight.

Much relieved by our separation, I went briskly home; sincerely, though somehow not very hopefully, praying that London might prove kind enough to hold us two without bringing us together.

CHAPTER XII.

THE season was fading when I returned to London. Even in our dull and barbarous district people were beginning to make ghastly affectation of going out of town; while in the streets which society and civilisation claimed for their own the windows were darkening one after another, much as the coloured lamps of an old-fashioned illumination, before the universal reign of gas had set in, used to fade and die towards morning.

Lilla had a rapid summary of news for me. "Nothing much" had occurred, as she phrased it; her uncle had not yet left town; he had had a quarrel with his daughters, and she had an idea that it was all about the Opera and Mademoiselle Reichstein. O, hadn't I heard? Mademoiselle Reichstein had made such a success! O, yes—splendid! But she had broken off her engagement rather suddenly, and she wanted to go to the other opera-house, and there was quite a turmoil about it; and Lilla believed there was going to be a lawsuit. But, however that might be, Mr. Lyndon was quite infatuated about her; and people would keep saying that he wanted to marry her; and his daughters were in such a way about it, and there was a row in the building, Lilla believed. She was quite delighted at the prospect of a "row" continuing and growing to be something serious, for she utterly detested Mr. Lyndon's daughters; and she was going to be introduced to Mademoiselle Reichstein.

"But if your uncle marries, Lilla, that will be rather a bad thing for you?"

"Yes; but I don't believe it will come to anything. I should think a woman so young, and with such a career before her, isn't going to marry a man who has daughters quite as old as herself and once and a half as tall. If I were she, I know that nothing on earth should induce me to do such a thing. O, how I envy her! How happy some people are! What success they have, and gifts, and beauty! And what a miserable life a girl like me is doomed to lead! Here in this wretched old den! I wonder how one can live through it. I never cross the bridge but I think how sad and dreary my life is, and how much I should like to drown myself, if I had the courage. *She* must be as happy as a queen. I envy her, and I admire her too."

" Have you seen her ?"

"No; her portrait only; and it was a wretched portrait too—a thing in a music-shop, with some rubbishy piece of music appended: but it made her beautiful and queenly, and sad too, I thought. But I am to see her. Is it possible you did not hear of her success down in the country ?"

" O yes, of course I did. But I am tired of all the singers who are everyone in turn to surpass Jenny Lind and Grisi, and who disappear in a season."

" But the town is ringing with her."

" Yes, so it was with Mademoiselle Johanna Wagner; so it was with no end of women. Where are they all now ?"

" Well, I don't know; but I have quite made up my mind that this one shall succeed and have a splendid career, and come to know me and be

very fond of me, and take me behind the scenes,
and have me in her box ; and please don't destroy
my delicious dream. I have not many pleasant
dreams here, I can tell you. I never saw success
in a living form face to face before; and pray
don't convince me that I am not really to see it
now. If you have come back cynical and out of
humour, pray go away again on your travels;
although we were precious lonely without you, I
can tell you that."

" Were you lonely without me ?"

" O yes, very. Mamma thought you would
never come back."

" And you, Lilla ?"

" Yes ; I too was very lonely."

" And you were glad when I came back ?"

" Glad ? Yes, surely. You don't suppose I
was not glad ?"

The frank look of kindly affectionate surprise
with which Lilla spoke these words had a warm-
ing, almost a thrilling influence on me. I think
I had begun of late to form a kind of vague idea
that Lilla might easily be induced to fall in love
with me. I certainly did not love her, and I
saw nothing in her manner towards me which

spoke of love. But we were so much thrown together, we were both so lonely, that I sometimes began to ask myself whether it would not be possible for me to descend from my pinnacle of sublime isolation, and lift her towards my heart.

I look back now upon myself and upon my ways at that time with the feeling which I suppose most people entertain towards their youth, curiously blended of regret and admiration and contempt. What a vain creature I was, and yet how stupidly timid and diffident! What a fool I was, and how convinced of my own wisdom! How miserable I was, and how happy! What an admiration I had for my own merits, and yet what a rapturous and servile gratitude I felt to any woman who seemed to cast a favouring eye upon me! I kept thinking complacently whether I really could accept Lilla's love, without asking myself whether any consideration on earth could induce her to accept me as a lover; and yet all the time I was filled with a sense of humiliating gratefulness to the girl for having condescended to be friendly and kindly to me. Of course I thought to myself, if I could make up my mind to come down from my clouds and try to love her, I must tell her openly, tragically, that I was a blighted being, that I had hardly any heart left to give, and so forth. Even then I had a faint doubt whether this would not be a little too much in the style of Dickens's Mr. Moddle, with whom I knew Lilla to be well acquainted; and what a pretty thing it would be, if she were only to burst out laughing at my lachrymose avowal!

Yet the moment was tempting; the situation became critical. Lilla had her levities and her faults, that was plain enough; only a lover's eye could be blind to them, and I was not a lover. But they could surely be ameliorated, eradicated gently by patience and superior wisdom—mine, *par exemple*. Who did not once believe himself capable of reforming anyone on whom he chose to try his hand? I am slow to believe in my own or anybody else's reforming capabilities now; but I suppose I then thought that, if I but condescended to attempt the task, I could remove all the weaknesses and defects from poor Lilla's nature, and replace them by some splendid grafts of earnestness and lofty purpose.

However this may be, Lilla's friendly admission that she was lonely in my absence had sent a strange, sweet vibration through me. When this conversation occurred, we were crossing St. James's-park. Thus far our roads lay together, and when there was a possibility of such companionship, we always took advantage of it. It was a beautiful evening, and the light of the setting sun threw a poetical glory over even the arid gravel and stunted trees of the park. It was a dangerous time and hour to walk with a pretty woman, and hear her tell you that she had been lonely in your absence.

I glanced at Lilla. Her eyes were downcast —only, I now believe, because the level rays of the evening sun threatened them—and there was a faint crimson on her cheeks. She was silent. I felt my soul dissolving in sentiment.

"Then you were really glad of my return, Lilla, and you thought of me in my absence?"

She looked up quickly, smilingly, perhaps just a little surprised.

"Thought of you? O yes, always! How could I help thinking of you?"

What I might have poured out in another second I am glad to say that I can never know. It would undoubtedly have been some idiotcy to

be bitterly regretted by myself afterwards; and, as
I now know, not likely to have caused her any
particular delight then, even if she had not
laughed at it. But she suddenly stopped in her
sentence, and caught me by the arm, and a
carriage drove past us from behind. Two ladies
were in it, and a gentleman, whose iron-gray hair
and purpling complexion I knew at a glance. I
only saw the bonnets of the ladies. Lilla bowed
to her uncle, and I saw her cheek redden.

"It's my uncle," she said; "and I know—I
am sure—one of the ladies with him is Mdlle.
Reichstein. I didn't even get a glimpse of her,
did you?"

"No; I only saw bonnets."

"O, I wish I had seen her! I am sure it's
she; I am so sorry! And he saw us. I don't
care a bit; in fact, I am delighted, because now it
will remind him of you; and I didn't like to speak
too much about you, or too often, because—"

And Lilla really blushed for the second time
that day.

But the blushing was useless now: the spell
was broken; my sublime self-devotion vanished.
Lilla's voice, and her evident first sensation of

something like doubt or shame at being seen in my companionship, and her raptures about Mdlle. Reichstein, were enough. How full of kindness for me her whole heart was, I could not but see; and I loved her in one way for that and other things; but the glamour of the moment was gone, and I left her when our ways divided at Pall Mall a free man, still faithful to my one memory and one love.

Two or three days passed away before an evening and an event came which I can never forget. I had been in town all day, and came home rather tired just after the last rays of a stormy sunset had sunk below the horizon of the low-lying region where we lived. My room, as I entered it, was in dusk; but I could see as I came in a letter for me standing on the chimney-piece. I went over apathetically and took it in my hand; but the sight of the inscription sent a fierce shock through me, and my head throbbed with a wild pain, born of surprise and sudden emotion. I knew that writing well. I put the letter down for a moment, just that my heart might beat less wildly, and my nerves become steady. Then I opened it, and read:

" Emanuel,—I have seen you again, and you did not know it. I was near you. After so many years, it was strange. I am glad we did not meet to speak. I only write this word to wish you may be happy always. Nothing is left but—greeting, and farewell.

" Christina."

I put the letter down and leaned on the chimney-piece. I was for a while incapable of thinking. I was literally stricken to the heart. We had been close to each other, and I had not seen her ! If the foolery of our modern days could have truth behind it, and a living man could really, by help of some spiritualistic incantations, be reached by the voice and affected by the presence of some loved being from another world, he might feel somewhat as I felt then, but without my bitterness. No voice reaching out of the shadow of the world that lies outside nature could have affected me with a more agonising sense of unavailable nearness and hopeless distance. Near to me— close to me—her very writing lying on my table— and no clue or trace by which a word of mine might reach her ! If I could but see her once—

but speak half-a-dozen words—but tell her of my
strong love! Was it not cruel thus to torture
me with such a message? Why not leave me to
my lonely struggle? I was comparatively happy;
I was almost contented; I had not forgotten her,
but she had become to me as the dead are, and I
had no hope. Bitterly did I now recall my first
knowledge of her departure, my first sense of her
loss, my first agony of uncertainty and torment.
Now all woke up again with keener pain, with a
deeper sense of tantalised and thwarted love.

Perhaps she too, like myself, is unhappy, is
struggling alone, and has sent out these few words
for the poor sake of reaching a friendly ear by
some means, as parting voyagers call a greeting to
distant friends upon the fading shore, although no
answer can reach them. Are we both, then, struggling unaided in this vast London? Has one city
held us all these years, and I never knew it? Is
she poor like me, and hopeless? Or is she married and happy; and having seen me at last by
chance, did she but look up for a moment and
think of the boy whom years ago she loved, and,
impelled by meaningless impulse, send him a
word of greeting and farewell? Have I lost her

utterly and for ever; or will some other message, more distinct than this, reach me yet, and guide me to her?

This thought for a while lighted up a hope, a sickly, flickering hope, within me. Perhaps, as she lives, is near me, has seen me, has sent me a message, her mere words do not mean what she feels, and I shall hear from her soon again, and we shall meet. I was somewhat weak of late from over-exertion. I think I must have been weak indeed, in mind as well as in body, when such a hope could inspire me for a moment. Well I knew that even when Christina loved me most, she loved success yet more; and what temptation could my future offer to such a spirit? I looked from the window, and the drear evening gloom made the flat and swampy places around, the mouldering houses, the blighted trees, look grayer and ghostlier than ever. Heavy rain was now beginning to fall, and the sky was all cloud and gloom. Nothing on earth could look more dreary to me than the prospect out of doors, except, indeed, the personal prospect which my soul fore-shadowed. Sad and heavy, like that mournful scene below — brightened by no ray of light, cheered by no pleasant sound — all dim, and misty, and gray. If I could find Christina, should I offer her a share of this one room, looking out on that swamp, and get her to canvass for pupils, who might learn music from her at sixpence a lesson, among the dirty children and the unfinished streets all around? I pictured her, as I saw so many women in the neighbourhood, struggling for mere life, with children crying round her, and cramping her very efforts to get them bread, that they might eat of it and live. Why, there is a peculiar expression graven on the faces of a certain class of women in London, which cuts the very heart to look at. And why should I expect better fortune for a woman doomed to be wife of mine? London garrets swarm with men infinitely better and more worthy of success than I, and yet on whom no gleam of fortune ever falls.

Once, it is true, I had more courage and more hope. But London struggle has something in it demoralising. No contrast in life can be more chilling and crushing than that of ideal London with actual London in such a case as mine. To ideal London we look in our ardour as the youth does to the battle, which he pictures as all thrill-

ing with the generous glory of strife, the rush of
the exhilarating charge, the clangour of the bugle,
the roar of the cannon, the cheers of the victor,
the honour and the wreath, or the noble, soldier-
like, dramatic death. Actual London is the slow,
cold camping on the wet earth, the swamp, malaria,
the ignoble hunger and thirst, the dull lying in
the trenches, the mean physical exhaustion, the
unrecognised, unrecorded disappearance. What
has become of the poor, raw, boyish recruit who
sank exhausted in the mud of the night march, or
was trampled to death in the retreat, or came back
with a broken constitution from the hospital, to
drag out a few obscure and miserable years at
home?

I seemed to myself to be like the most ignoble and the most unhappy of them. Should
I wish Christina to share such fortunes—to become entangled in such a career?

Or if she were prosperous, could I beg of her
prosperity, and be warmed meekly in the sun of
her success?

This last idea was so hateful to me, that I
strode passionately up and down the room to
banish it, and felt inclined to invoke curses on

myself for the meanness which even allowed it to have an instant's possession of my mind.

Ah, no! She is lost, lost for ever! Whether she lives in light or in gloom, she is lost alike to me! I could not brighten the gloom. I will never stoop to be illumined — a pitiful, poor, human planet—by the light. I take her farewell literally—and farewell!

A tap at the door broke in upon my lonely thoughts. The disturbance was grateful to me; any intruder would have been welcome at such a time. It was not an intruder, however, who sought to be admitted, but Lilla Lyndon. Her looks showed her to be brimful of some intelligence. She was dressed as if she had only just come in, and her cheeks and curls were sparkling with rain-drops.

"Do you know where I have been?" she began. "But you need not try to guess, for you never could succeed. I have been to see Mademoiselle Reichstein with my uncle."

"Indeed! Do you like her?"

"Yes, immensely. She is delightful, I think, and so good, and very handsome. You don't seem at all interested in her. Wait a bit, I have something to tell you which will interest you, cold-hearted philosopher as you are. But stop— are you not well?"

"Yes, Lilla, quite well."

"You don't look like it, then. I'll send mamma to talk to you presently. Perhaps I have something to tell you which will help you to get better."

"I am not ill, indeed, Lilla."

"Well, let me get on with my news. My uncle came with me; but after a while he left me with Mademoiselle Reichstein, and I remained for more than an hour, and she sang to me delightfully; and she was so kind and good, and seemed to take such an interest in me, you can't think; only I put it down in my own mind to the account of the interest she takes in my revered uncle, who, if he's not very young, at least has plenty of money. However, she took such an interest in me, that, when we were alone, I came to the point which I had at heart all through— and I spoke to her about you. Ah! now you begin at last to think it worth while listening to what I say."

Yes, I must own that even while she spoke a

strange boding thrill passed through me, and I held my breath in a kind of agony.

"I can tell you I spoke highly of you, and told her how fond mamma was of you, and I too. I do wonder what you would have thought if you only knew what I allowed her to think in order to persuade her to take an interest in you."

"What did you allow her to think?"

"I declare you are quite hoarse, Emanuel. You are in for a bad cold."

"No, no, Lilla; do pray go on."

"Well, I had rather you guessed at my pious fraud. I didn't exactly say the false word, but I am afraid I gave it out somehow. She asked me a question about you, and about my interest in you, and I allowed her to think—O, there, I am quite ashamed of myself; and I suppose a girl better brought up than I would not have done such a thing for all the world. But I have not been brought up well, and I never could stick at trifles to serve a friend—and in fact, Mr. Temple, I think I allowed Mdlle. Reichstein to believe that you and I were engaged, and only waited to be married until you had made your way a little. There's the whole truth out; and all I can say

in my own defence is, that if I had not as much
esteem for you and confidence in you, Emanuel
Temple, as if you were my own brother, I would
never, never, bad as I am, have been guilty of anything so unblushing and unwomanly. There now,
how dreadfully miserable you look ! I really don't
see that you need be so utterly humiliated and
ashamed—I daresay Mdlle. Reichstein did not
think any the worse of *you*, whatever she may
have thought of me."

I was hardly conscious of any meaning in these
latest words of hers. I was not thinking of humiliation, or of what she had said on my behalf.
One thought, one conjecture, was swelling up
within me so as to flood and drown every other
feeling.

"I feel greatly obliged to you, Lilla, greatly
obliged," was all I could say.

"And you look it too."

"But Mdlle. Reichstein ?"

"Well, Mdlle. Reichstein was most kind and
amiable. She sat quite silent and thoughtful for
a while, perhaps considering how best she could
lend a helping hand. It must be a far more difficult matter than I thought, for she put her hand

over her eyes, and remained thinking quite a time. Then she kissed me, and wished me all happiness. I felt like a shamefaced and convicted liar. Yes, she wished happiness to *me*—to me, the most unhappy, discontented, lonely, hopeless creature under the sun!—and then she sat down and wrote a letter to Princeps—the great Princeps himself, the manager of the Italian Opera—and I saw that she tore up two or three copies before she was satisfied with the writing (I believe half these *prima donnas* can't spell); and then she read it to me. It was all about you, and making it a personal favour to help you—very strongly put, I can tell you. I offered to post it as I came along, in order to be quite sure that it went; for she said Princeps was not in London now, and it would be impossible for you to see him for some weeks; and she asked me—but this I really ought not to tell you."

"Tell me all, Lilla—all, all!"

"Good gracious, how hoarse you are! Well, she is so kind and thoughtful that she begged me not to tell you anything about the whole affair. People don't always like, she said, to think that they are being helped along, and it would be better

if you supposed that you were being sought out—
for you will be sought out—for your own merit
only. Was not that considerate and delicate?
But I know you have no such nonsense about
you, and I want you to know how kind she is,
and so I have told you, though I promised I
wouldn't—the second fib to-day on your account,
Mr. Emanuel Temple. O, that reminds me that
I must have let drop your full name somehow, for
she seemed quite to know it."

O, God in heaven! I stood up and clenched
my hands.

"And now I think that's all; except that she
gave me her picture, and I think her so beautiful!
O, how I do wish she would marry my uncle!
Why, what is the matter with you?"

"Show me the picture, Lilla."

She sought in her pocket, then in the bosom
of her dress. I stood trembling with excitement,
keen pains again darting through my forehead, the
square of light made by the window rising and
falling before my eyes.

"Surely I can't have lost it? No, here it is.
Is she not beautiful? Such a mass of hair, and
all her own too."

I took the picture from her. It was one of the old-fashioned daguerreotypes now as completely gone out of the world as Miss La Creevy's enamelled miniatures. When I first seized it and gazed upon it, the light so fell as to blot it out completely, and my impatient eyes only looked upon a blank space. Forcing down my emotion, I brought it to the window, held it in the proper light, and then—

"Lilly, my dear; Lilly, my own," broke in, thank Heaven! the plaintive tones of Mrs. Lyndon.

"Yes, mamma; what's up?"

"My child, you musn't stay in your wet things. Come down, dear; I want you."

"O, what does it matter! Yes, I am coming. —Keep the picture for the present, Emanuel, and fall in love with it if you can. I would, I know, if I were a man. I'll send up for it presently."

Thank God she was gone! I could not have endured her presence much longer without betraying my feelings by a wild explosion. Yes; it was as I expected—the face in the daguerreotype was the face of Christina Braun. Her dream, then, had come true. She had done her part. She was successful.

Ah, God! I hardly needed to look at the poor little daguerreotype, or to struggle against the growing dusk for a clear sight of that face. By some force of ineffable conviction, the moment Lilla came into the room and spoke of Mdlle. Reichstein, I guessed the truth, of which I had never dreamed before. Often as she had talked to me of Mdlle. Reichstein, the notion had never before occurred to my mind that the successful *prima donna* could be my lost Christina. But the letter —the few lines I had myself received that night— brought her back into my mind as a living reality again, and I knew the whole truth before my eyes or ears had any evidence of it.

Yes, I am unable to account for it, but I knew it to be the fact that the moment Lilla entered the room and named the name of Mdlle. Reichstein, it came on me with the convincing force of a revelation that she and Christina Braun were one, and that I had lost Christina for ever.

She was successful. Did I not know that she would be some time? And yet it came on me now with a surprise which was like agony. Like agony? Nay, it was agony; for it severed us more, far more, than death could do. She was lost, lost to me. The one hope which had lighted my lonely life so long had utterly gone out. When, years ago, I used to hold her to my heart and talk to her of her future success, I always spoke of it as conjoined with my own, as the crown of a common happiness. In how many hours of love and hope, in how many happy walks under the summer stars, in how many silent dreams, had we pictured that triumph for her and for me! We were to make our way together through life, to become successful and famous, and then to come back and amaze the little town, which we magniloquently declared did not know us. Or, if we did not succeed—for I at least had my moments of distrust and doubt—I always looked forward to our struggling and perhaps suffering together, still happy because together. Even our sudden and strange separation I had sometimes regarded as a glorious self-sacrifice, to be crowned and rewarded some day. Many a night had I returned sick of heart and weary of foot to my London lodging, and, musing over the hours of happiness, love, and hope I had once enjoyed, been cheered and brightened by the thought that perhaps my struggles here were working in unseen coöperation with her to-

wards the same end. There was still at least a
link of companionship, and a hope that it might
draw us together one day. As my eyes were fixed
upon the pale, far-off star of my hope, it was some
consolation and joy to think that wherever she
might be, her eyes and her soul were turned towards it too.

And now, behold, one half at least of our most
ardent prayer has been fulfilled. She has won all
we dreamed of and hoped for. Why do I not re-
joice? I was to have been the first to hail her
triumph, and now I greet it with agony and shame;
as if her success were my defeat and humiliation.
And it is so. I feel that no poverty, no failure, no
temporary isolation under the pressure of misfortune could raise such barriers between her and me
as this fatal granting of one half our prayer. Poor
people may become less poor, or they may grow
familiar with poverty and learn to endure it, or
they may conquer its pain by the strength of love
and hope. But this revelation of her success has
sounded the last of love and hope for me. Why,
all these years that I have been picturing her heart
as turning eternally towards mine, and panting for
reunion, she has been simply making her way in

the world! She has run over some of the most
thrilling chords of human experience, she has won
every height to which she aspired; while I have
been removing from one town to another, my
greatest triumph to exchange a garret for a small
back-parlour. I feel crushed down by grief and
shame. She must despise me. She *has* actually
patronised me! The great singer has granted, at
the humble petition of a poor girl, a letter of introduction, to help a struggling and obscure poor
devil to an engagement in a chorus. I had imagined many a renewal of our former days, many a
first greeting after our long separation, many a
meeting under all conceivable circumstances of joy
and of sorrow; but I had thought of nothing like
this. I had forgotten to picture myself as a broken-
down beggar petitioning for help; and her as a
triumphant and splendid *prima donna* granting
me the favour at the solicitude of a wealthy and
elderly lover.

Why, it seems but last week that she wrote
those letters I keep in my trunk, full of such
love, and tenderness, and admiration—admiration
for me! and now I am her debtor for a letter of
introduction, obtained through the importunity of

Lilla Lyndon and the influence of her rich uncle,
in order that, if I am well conducted, I may receive perhaps an engagement in the chorus of the
Italian Opera! I wonder she did not send me a
small present of money! But perhaps if I obtain
a place as chorus-singer through her influence,
and conduct myself properly, and never appear to
recognise her, she may assist me in some other
way too. She may, for example, give Lilla the
making of some of her fine stage-dresses, or even
the place of her own dressing-room attendant;
and if Lilla and I get married, the great *prima
donna* may kindly become godmother to one of
our children! Ah, but if the *prima donna* should
marry Lilla's rich uncle, then indeed something
better could doubtless be done for Lilla than to
marry her to a wretch like me! In the bitterness of my heart it seemed as if my love for
Christina had turned into hate.

I was only aroused from the depth of bitter
thought into which I had plunged by my own
voice—by the sound of a deep, involuntary, irrepressible groan, wrung from me by agony of love,
disappointment, shame, hate. In the silent, darkling room the groan sounded hollow and ghostly,

as in a vault of death. It aroused me as a dreamer is sometimes awakened by the sound of his own babble or laughter.

I started up with the resolve to do something. Yes, there was something I could and would do— I would see her face to face. I would go to her, speak to her, ask of her how she dared to insult me with her patronage. I meant no appeal to the love of the old days; no poor and pitiful plaint, no ghastly effort to recall the dead past from the grave. No; we are parted for ever; and I accept my doom, and make no complaint. Only she shall know that I want no patronage, and will stoop to accept none. Let her spare me that. For the sake even of the old days which she has forgotten, for the sake of the love which I would not now have her renew if I could—no, by Heaven!—let her spare me that! Let me but see her, speak to her, vindicate to her face my pride and my independence; and perhaps—perhaps I then can better bear with life.

Filled with this thought, I went downstairs and tapped at the door of Mrs. Lyndon's room, endeavouring meanwhile to still the fierce beatings of my heart, and to keep some control over

my voice and manner. Lilla's voice called to me
to come in. I had hoped to find her mother
there, thinking I could get on better in ordinary
conversation if there were three of us at it, than
in mere *tête-à-tête* with my quick and sharp-eyed
Lilla. But I could hear Mrs. Lyndon at work at
some cookery-business below in the kitchen, and
Lilla was alone. Must I confess the truth? I
almost hated the poor girl for her well-meant,
kindly, luckless interference on my behalf.

When I entered, Lilla was apparently in a
condition of great comfort and happiness. She
was lying, or rather huddled up, on a little sofa,
which was drawn over to the table, on which a
lamp threw a soft and pleasant light, and she was
reading a novel. Lilla loved novel-reading. She
had a great shawl gathered cosily around her,
covering her from neck to feet—indeed, I think
her feet must have been coiled up under her,
sultana fashion, for greater comfort; for the
night, though in summer, had turned a little
chilly, and Lilla had been out in the rain on my
behalf. In fact, the poor girl had probably taken
off her wet dress, and had wrapped herself in a
shawl as an easy substitute. I know she always

liked to get the room to herself when she had a novel to read, for her mother was a dreadfully irritating person at such a time, full as she always was of anxious questions and perplexing recommendations. So Lilla was evidently very happy; and as she looked up at me with her beaming eyes, and her pretty head peeping above the great enveloping shawl, in which the whole of her figure was lost, she must have been very charming to any eyes but mine. In my bitter, diseased, distracted state of mind, it irritated me to see her looking so cosy, and pretty, and happy. I felt much as an angry man feels when, striding moodily to his fire, he stumbles over the sleek, contented, purring cat that lies basking on the hearthrug.

"Have you brought me my picture?" asked my happy Lilla.

There was an intense odour of savoury frying below, which I grieve to think must have conduced a good deal to the happiness of this good girl's mind. Her harmless and comfortable little sensuousness was regaled and propitiated on the odour from below, like the goodwill of the old gods on the steam of the fat sacrifice.

"Yes, I have brought it."

" Isn't it lovely ?"

" Very."

" How chillingly you say that ! Men have no taste ; and I am sure it is all nonsense to say that *we* don't admire pretty women more than you do. I am quite in love with that face and hair; and you don't seem to care a straw about it."

" Well, I think, I believe I should like to keep it a little longer, just to study it, Lilla, and understand it a little, if you don't object, and will leave it to me only for to-night."

Had I been asking Lilla to elope with me, or to steal her uncle's purse for me, I could not have preferred the request in more awkward and stammering accents. My pretty one gathered herself into something like a more upright posture on the sofa, and looked at me with all the inquisitive, penetrating brightness of her eyes.

" O yes, surely. I am very glad you want to look at it a little more, for I should be so pleased if you came to admire it as I do. But I don't understand you to-night, somehow — you don't seem like yourself."

" All the better if I seem like somebody else— anybody else, Lilla."

" Nonsense ! Tell me one thing, and speak truly, and without any evasion or chaff—are you at all sick ? Because, if you are, I really must set mamma at you ; but if not—I mean if there's anything wrong that isn't sickness, or catching cold or that sort of thing—mamma would be only a bore and a plague to you, and you had better be let alone. Tell me frankly, do you wish to be let alone ?"

" Indeed, Lilla, I am perfectly well."

" Then you want to be let alone ?"

" I see you have been reading. What's the novel ?"

" O, a charming thing—so beautiful and poetic ; only it is so sad—*The Improvisatore ;* do you know it ? by Hans Christian Andersen, the Danish novelist. I have just been reading such a touching passage. The hero was in love with an actress, you know, a beautiful creature, and they got separated somehow—through a mistake entirely—and he never saw her for years and years after ; and when at last he came to see her again (on the stage) for the first time since their separation, she was quite withered and old, and her beauty was all gone. It is such a touching chapter. All her youth was gone, and her good looks, and she was old."

"Even beautiful actresses, Lilla, must get old."

"But why were they separated? It is too sad; I don't like stories that are so sad."

"Yet you read it, and think it charming."

"Yes, I can't help being delighted with it. But it is too melancholy. I can't bear to think of their long, long separation, and of her being old and withered when at last they met. I suppose such things do happen?"

"I suppose they do. I think I have heard of separations, or read of them perhaps."

Again Lilla looked curiously at me, and she put down the book.

"Speaking of beautiful actresses, Lilla," I said, with a supreme effort to be light and careless, "does your beautiful friend, Mademoiselle Reichstein, live far from here; and did you walk home through all the rain?"

"Yes. It was rather a distance; but I didn't mind in the least."

"Did you tell me where it was? I quite forget."

"In Jermyn-street, just opposite an hotel—I don't know the number—a very nice place. Some elderly person lives with her—a companion or friend, or something of the kind."

Mrs. Lyndon just then came up, and pressed me to stay with them and have supper; but I told them I had to go into town again; I had forgotten to see somebody with whom I had an appointment, and must try to find him now, late though it was.

I got out of the house somehow. It was now a streaming wet night, and I tramped long enough before I could find an omnibus going my way. When I got at last to the Haymarket, it was half-past ten o'clock, and I was very wet. An appropriate hour, a pleasant condition, in which to present myself as a visitor at the door of a lady's boudoir! I felt a grim and bitter satisfaction in the thought of my forlorn and wretched appearance. I almost wished that I were in rags, that I might be the more savagely in contrast with her condition—that I might stand in utter wretchedness before her, and fierce in my desolate independence, fling back her patronage and her written vows of love. I longed to stand before her and say, "Look at this ruined and hopeless wretch,

this ragged beggar! This was your lover! There
are your written vows of love for him, and thus he
flings them back to you, with the offer of your
queenly patronage. Pauper though he may be,
you shall not dare to befriend him. Let the beggar die. He shall not, at least, be fed with the
crumbs that fall from your table!"

I found the house without difficulty. A waiter
standing at the door of Cox's Hotel told me at
once where Mdlle. Reichstein the singer lodged.
The drawing-room windows were all dark. In my
savage mood I felt bitterly disappointed at the
prospect of not seeing her after all. I knocked at
the door.

Mdlle. Reichstein had gone, the servant told
me.

Gone where?

She didn't quite know; somewhere abroad: to
Paris, she thought. She went that evening by the
night-mail.

Could she inquire, and find out for me?

She went into the house, but came back to say
she really could not get to know. Mdlle. Reichstein had gone certainly to the Continent with her
maid and the other lady; to Paris first, probably;

but the lady of the house thought she was very likely going somewhere farther away.

Would she return here soon?

O no, certainly not. Not before next season.

That was all. I could find out nothing else.

I turned away from the door with a sickening sense of disappointment and hopelessness. Ah, only the Power above could tell—I surely could not—how much of a secret, passionate longing to see her again, for any purpose, on any terms, was mingled with my fierce resolve to confront her, and to fling her back her agonising proffer of service.

I turned into the glaring, chattering, hell-lighted Haymarket—a stricken, hopeless wretch. Despite the rain, that still came down pretty heavily, this Babel of harlotry was all alive and aflame with its beastly gaiety.

I strode my way along with head down and reckless demeanour, careless whom I jostled. Blindly I struck up against somebody, who first drew back and swore at me, and then, seizing me by my arm, exclaimed:

" My heroic preserver! would you overturn rudely the friend who longed to meet you? What, not know me ? How bears himself *ce gros militaire ?*"

Of course I knew him. It was my confounded friend of Dover.

" I told you we should meet again," he said; " I don't know that it's quite a fortunate thing for you; but we are all in the hands of the destinies. You see Heaven would bring us to together."

" The devil rather, I should think," was my grumbled answer.

" Let it be the devil, dear young friend, if you have faith only in him. It cheers me to find that you believe even in the devil; youth is so unbelieving nowadays. But you are cynical tonight, which means, I daresay, that *she* is faithless or out of humour. Bear up, and let us be merry. Look here : you are wet, so am I; you are out of sorts, so am I. Let us spend a jovial hour together, and mingle our tears."

I could have welcomed just then the society of Satan. He not appearing, I suffered my other friend to put his arm in mine and lead me away.

CHAPTER XIII.

GOODBOY'S BROTHER.

I AWOKE next morning with a fierce headache, a deep sense of moral debasement, and a still deeper sense of savage satisfaction in my own degradation. I contemplated a sort of moral suicide. It seemed like an act of vengeance on her who had loved me and now cast me away, thus to crush and ruin the nature of the being to whom she once turned in love.

I am not fond of oral confessions or moral self-exposures, and therefore I hasten to say that my abasement—this my first abasement—would have been in the eyes of any ordinary Haymarket *habitué* a very small affair indeed. I drank too much that night—and for the first time—that was all. As the next day wore on, and I grew better accustomed to the quite new sense of shame, I frankly told Lilla Lyndon of my excess of the previous night, and she did not seem to think a

great deal about the matter. I was, on the whole,
rather disappointed that she took it so com-
posedly. Moral suicide, after all, seemed a commonplace process.

Yet Lilla looked grave and frowned warningly
at me when she saw me going out again about the
same hour that night.

" Once and away," she observed, " mayn't be
very bad ; but take care, Emanuel, or we shall
all be sorry."

I was going into the Haymarket, where I had
pledged myself to meet my friend again. A queer
sort of fascination drew me towards him ; and
some words he had let drop the previous night—
words I now remembered but faintly—had keenly
quickened my interest in him. When we parted,
I promised to meet him in the colonnade of the
Opera-house at nine o'clock ; and at nine I was
there. Very soon after, he made his appearance,
and I noted at once that the appearance he made
was considerably changed : he was all new, from
hat to boots, and his gloves were of dainty
lavender.

" Surprised at the change, my dear young
friend ?" he observed complacently. " Don't be

ashamed to confess that you have been looking at me with eyes of wonder and admiration. I am not susceptible of offence; and the homage of the ingenuous can never displease the serene soul. I was very shabby-looking yesterday, and now I am not so. I do not blush to confess that the change is not wholly owing to my own merit or industry."

"You told me you were a great hand at billiards, and indeed I saw some evidence of your skill last night."

"So you did. I think I rather astonished you and the others too. But it isn't that. You see me in the sunshine of a prosperity the source of which you could never guess. Indeed, it upsets the creed of half a lifetime with me. I should never have believed it, were I not a living proof of the fact. Listen, youth; and, if prematurely given over, as you doubtless are, to cynicism, learn now a new and refreshing lesson of life. I am a living evidence of a woman's gratitude."

"Glad to hear it."

"But you don't seem sufficiently startled. Did you ever find a woman true and grateful?"

"No, by God!"

"Aha, there you are with your bears! I thought as much. There was good earnest in that vow. Will you come with me to my lodgings? Yes, I *have* lodgings near at hand; that's part of the mystery. Come with me. I long to be a host once more, especially to one who, like myself, so evidently belongs to the brotherhood of poor devils."

We walked along Jermyn-street. When we passed the house where *she* so lately lived, my eyes turned unconsciously towards it and fixed themselves on it. He too was looking that way: it was on the other side of the street. He noticed my gaze.

"How odd!" he observed; "you are looking at No. 15—I am looking at No. 15. It can't have the same story for you and for me. Did you catch a sight of some pretty Mary-Jane in smart cap and ribbons? Frivolous youth!"

Frivolous youth made no answer, and indeed remained silent until we had reached Bury-street, and gone some way down it.

My companion stopped at a door, took out a latch-key, opened the door with it, and waved to me with an air of gracious lordliness to enter.

"My lodgings," he exclaimed; "second-floor front."

The second-floor front was a small handsomely-furnished sitting-room, with bedroom *en suite*. My friend lighted a lamp, and motioned me to an arm-chair.

"I took these rooms at once to-day," he said, "on receiving the unexpected mark of gratitude of which I spoke to you. They are plain but commodious. The engravings on the wall are not remarkable as works of art. Let me see: 'The Happy Days of Charles the First,' simple inanity. Her gracious Majesty on horseback in military habit. Well, well, let us be always loyal, however the court-painter may try us. 'Phœbe,' a young woman simpering over a fowl of some sort —dove, I presume—and apparently wearing only her chemise, which she has omitted to fasten round the neck: idiotcy! No matter. There's a piano, you see, which is something. Do you love music?"

"Love it, no! No more, that is. Live by it."

"Live by it, and not love it! No, you can't! Not even in this cursed day of quacks and shams

and successful Jack Puddings, can any man live
by music who does not love it. I only wish the
converse of the proposition held equally, and that
everyone who loved it could live by it. Were
that so, some people might have been more virtuous and independent, perhaps, than they are.
Now, my young friend, whose name I have not
even yet the honour of knowing, but shall presently,
perhaps, ask to be favoured with—there is brandy,
there is water, and yonder are cigars. I am going
to sing a little, but smoke if you will; it can't put
my pipe out."

He sat down to the piano, his queer little legs
hardly touching the ground, and his long arms
spreading over the instrument like the wings of
some ungainly bird. One could hardly expect
much sweet music from so ridiculous-looking a
form, surmounted by a curly black wig; but he
played with no common skill and with quite uncommon feeling and fervour. Presently he sang,
in full, sweet, and solemn tones, the hymn,
"Lord, remember David." Strangely pathetic,
deep, and passionate sounded that mournful appeal as it issued from the lips of this singular
and scoffing little creature. I own, too, that it

touched me quite as much as it puzzled me ; so profound seemed the sincerity with which the prayer and the plaint went up in that tender, thrilling voice.

" Lord, remember David ; teach him to know Thy ways !" Every word seemed to come from him with a pathetic, passionate earnestness, so deep that one could almost for the time imagine he heard the half-despairing utterance of some generous and noble nature crying out for strength to battle against temptation, and for light to see in the world's foul darkness. I dreaded the close of the hymn, so much did I shrink from the contrast of levity or profanity with which I felt sure he would instantly follow it. But I was mistaken. He sat silent a moment or two when he had finished, and then jumped up from the piano and walked up and down the room. After a while I could hear him repeating to himself some of the words of the prayer in a low tone, as if it refreshed him to dwell on them.

" Now then," he said at last, " you who live on music, but, I think you said, don't care a curse about it, give us a musical blasphemy—I mean, of course, a song from unenthusiastic lips. Come

along; make no apologies or pretexts. I daresay
I have heard a hundred better singers before now,
so you need not stand on ceremony."

I sang something for him, accompanying myself. He stood behind me the while, and now and
then uttered a sort of growl of satisfaction, or
grunt of discontent.

"Ah, I thought so," he observed when I had
done; " yes, I felt sure I could not be mistaken.
It *was* you, then, I heard at the Dover concert,
Mr. Emanuel Temple! Well, Temple, I've heard
a good many worse singers than you, and a few
better. I think you ought to get on, though I do
fancy somehow that you want soul. But I should
say, with training and cultivation, and the advice
of qualified critics—like myself, for example—
you ought to make your way, Temple. I advise
you to stick to it, Temple. I decline to offer you
the blessing of an old man, Temple; first, because
I don't admit being old; and next, because I fear
my blessing would be like that of the priest in the
story, and worth considerably less than a farthing.
But I have prophesied of singers before now, and
prophesied correctly. I was hinting to you just
now of that rare and strange thing, a woman's

gratitude, and the romantic story is a story of a singer."

The glance I had seen him give at the windows which were lately Christina's, and the words he let fall immediately after, had aroused my curiosity. But I thought I had observed enough of his perverse and eccentric little nature to know that the more readily I displayed my curiosity the less inclined would he be to gratify it; so I affected an air of supreme cynicism, and coolly said :

" Then you expect me to believe in woman's gratitude ? Thank you ; but I really can't oblige you so far, and I have no faith in romantic stories."

" Nothing amuses me," he replied, " so much as the pert affectation of cynicism in brats of boys. You know very well, Temple, that if you left your real nature to itself, it would be rather credulous and soft than otherwise. Do you know now, that you struck me from the first as a good-natured and simple sort of fellow—an honest young spooney, in fact ; a lad that any smart girl might turn round her finger—a being doomed by nature to be married to a woman who will assume the wearing of the breeches as her natural right? That is quite my idea of you, Temple ; give you my word, as a candid friend and admirer."

" Well, but without occupying ourselves in the discussion of my moral organisation, what of your romantic story, and your grateful woman ?"

" You want to hear it, evidently."

" Not very particularly ; but if you insist—"

" Well, here it is. When I came to London the other day, and while yet casting about for the best way to torment my nearest relatives and raise some money, I devoted myself to *flâner* a little on *the* side of Regent-street, thinking of the old days, Temple, when I too was a club lounger and a man about town, and so on. I happened to glance into a photographer's, and there I saw a photograph of a singer, the singer of the season, the woman the two Opera-houses have been squabbling about, you know."

" Yes. Reichstein."

" Reichstein, of course. In a moment I recognised her as an old friend, Temple."

" Of yours ? She,—Mdlle. Reichstein—an old friend of yours !"

" Why not ? What are you glowering at ?

She's not an old friend of yours, I suppose; and even if she is, you needn't look daggers at *me*. Did I say an old friend of mine? Why, man, I discovered her, I invented her, I created her! I crossed the Channel with her years ago, when she was a poor little thing going to Paris, and hoping to get on to Italy; and I took quite a paternal liking to her; quite paternal, Temple, I can assure you; and for the good reason that she wouldn't allow of any other sort of liking; and I introduced her in Paris to an Italian fellow whom I knew; a fellow who was mad on two things — Music and Italian Revolution; and he quite took her up; and I only saw her once after in Milan, where he was having her drilled for the Scala. That, too, is four or five years ago; and to tell you the honest truth, Temple, I never thought of the little thing from that day to the day when I saw her portrait here in this den of thieves."

" Did you go to see her?"

" Well, I did call; but she didn't happen to be in; and I was not very sorry perhaps; for, as you can testify, my gifted vocalist, I was not quite in splendid trim about that time. But I

left a letter with a mild reminder of my early
services and a warm congratulation upon her brilliant success, to which it was gracefully hinted
that my artistic insight had not a little con-
tributed.   Then there came an oblique, pathetic
intimation that Fortune had not perhaps been
quite so favourable to myself; and, in short, I
am afraid it was conveyed more or less vaguely
that gratitude and sympathy might not unreason-
ably take the form of an early and liberal remittance."

I had hard work to keep down my rising disgust and contempt.

"And the remittance came?" I said, to say
something, as I saw he was looking towards me,
with his head on one side and his little beady
black eyes twinkling inquiringly.

"Yes, the remittance came, and it was liberal;
so liberal in fact that I have put off for the present opening the campaign I am prepared to
undertake.   So you perceive, Temple, that there
are women who can be grateful; perhaps I should
rather say that there are men so happily endowed
as to be capable of exciting the sentiment of
gratitude in woman's breast.   Between ourselves,

the service I rendered was not very great; for I
had actually at the time a sort of general and
roving commission from my friend the Italian
revolutionary to look out for fine fresh voices
wherever they could be picked up — he had a
mania for establishing an artistic *parc aux cerfs*
of young voices—only artistic and vocal, Temple,
nothing more ; he was a very Bayard or Scipio
in that way; and I simply sent the girl to him,
and thought no more about the matter. What
of that ? It only makes the gratitude more touching. It is a noble and a holy thing, you know,
to call up such a feeling ; that sentiment in the
woman's breast is cheaply bought by her at the
money."

" In fact, you place her under a fresh obli-
gation ?"

" Well, as you put it so, yes."

" And found perhaps a claim hereafter for
another remittance ?"

" That is your sneer, I daresay. No, my
scornful young friend, I think I shall be content
with that much from that quarter. Let me tell
you, however, to show how little I value your
feeble-minded insinuation, that I am one of those

who are rather proud to be relieved by the soft and generous hand of woman. I think history records that John duke of Marlborough, and other great men, acknowledged a similar sentiment, or at least acted on it. Nature is all symbolic, Temple. Whence do we derive our earliest sustenance? From woman's generous bosom. Go to, then; the meaning of Nature's beautiful parable must be evident to all true and poetic hearts. Mine is essentially a poetic nature; yours I perceive is not; you look at the bare rude fact of my pocketing the young woman's money, and do not see the delightful illustration of Nature's noblest and oldest purpose which it symbolises. What's the matter with you?"

"I have not been quite well lately; but—"

"Drink brandy, Temple; drink again."

"Do you know whether—whether this lady, Mdlle. Reichstein, is married?"

"Not I. How should I know; and what do I care? Very likely she is; they all get married, these people. The flag of matrimony is a very convenient emblem."

I got up to go away; his talk was hateful to me; and yet I clung to any feeble hope that I might extract some knowledge about her past life and her probable future.

" Do you know where she is gone ?"

" Russia, I believe ; but I am not certain. Somebody told me that some rich Londoner, a member of parliament and patron of the drama —I don't know him, but, as Charles Lamb said, ' d— him at a venture'—was always to be seen hanging after her, and making rather an idiot of himself."

" Yes, I have heard of that," I interposed very incautiously ; " and I know who it is — a Mr. Lyndon."

" What did you say ?" exclaimed the little creature, leaping from the chair in which he sat, and standing upright before me. " What name did you give ?"

" Lyndon—a Mr. Lyndon, a member of the House !"

" Earth and hell ! Tommy Goodboy ! Tommy Goodboy himself ! Of all the hypocrites of this most hypocritical age, Tommy Goodboy is the greatest hypocrite. Among all the scoundrels in an age of scoundrelism, no scoundrel like Tommy Goodboy. Look at me, Temple ! I am Goodboy's victim : Goodboy stands in my shoes ; Goodboy wallows in my money! He is the head of the family, the respectable citizen, the model man, the patron of every charity, the Mæcenas of art; and I am the ruffian, the outcast, the billiard-room hanger-on, the frightful example!"

An idea at last began to dawn upon me as to the identity of my queer friend. Were these, then, the two faces I had seen vaguely and tantalisingly shadowed in his? Lilla's face and Mr. Lyndon's? Is this creature, this half-crazed sensualist, this selfish loafer, this wretch living on alms and extorted money, this combination of Hircius and Spungius, my poor, pretty, kindly Lilla's father ?

He was now walking up and down the room, throwing his arms wildly about like a little madman. I went up to him as gently and kindly as I could.

"You, then," I said, "are the elder brother of Mr. Lyndon ?"

"Who the devil else do you think I am ? Do you suppose I am proud of being that cold-hearted, sneaking humbug's brother ? Yes; I am his brother—the brother whom he cheated out of house and home, out of his father's favour, out of his inheritance, out of everything that could make life worth having. Was I an idle, good-for-nothing scapegrace? Of course I was. But what was he? All that I did openly and recklessly, he did cunningly and underhand. How did he ruin me at last? By betraying to my father the one good thing I ever did in all my life. It's as true as light, Temple. My father cut me off without a rap because I had been d—d fool enough to marry a pretty girl instead of seducing her. Whatever misfortune may happen to you in life, Temple, never do a virtuous action. Be warned in time by me. When I die, or hang myself, if there can by any means be raised money enough to set up a tombstone over me, let my epitaph describe me as the man whom Respectability and Virtue outlawed and robbed, because he had once in his life—only just once—failed to behave like a scoundrel."

I was on the point of blurting out some hasty words which would have admitted my knowledge of Lyndon's wife and daughter. Fortunately, however, I restrained myself in time, and recollected how more than doubtful it was whether

they would be the better for any indiscretion which
put such a creature on their track. Poor, poor
Lilla! with her good heart, her sweet kindly nature, her harmless vanities, and at least not un-
natural hopes and aspirings, to think that this
unfortunate and worthless wretch, whose chief or
sole excuse seemed to be his half-crazed eccentricity, should be her father! I always fancied
that the poor girl cherished in her secret heart
some fond romantic hope that the lost mysterious
father might one day reappear, redeemed, peni-
tent, and splendid, to claim his daughter and lead
her into the sphere which she thought her right-
ful place. I know that she always regarded her
father as some brilliant aristocrat, who had stepped
down from his high rank for love of her poor
mother—some Egmont or Leicester, to whom
Mrs. Lyndon was the Clara or Amy Robsart; and
he filled her imagination even in his fall rather
as an archangel ruined than as any commonplace
sinner. I know—she often hinted as much to
me—that she secretly yearned for him, and waited
for him to come some day and redeem her from
poverty and meanness, and the society of petty
cares and small intelligences; and to bring her

to a sphere where there should be bright surroundings, and ease and luxury, and a life with
many tints in it, and vivid conversation, and books
worth reading, and men who could pay graceful
homage and whom one could marry, and women
well-dressed and vivacious and lovely. Often I
had thought to myself, in my odd moods of whimsical melancholy, that Lilla's phantom father and
my phantom Christina beguiled and befooled us
both alike, and to as little purpose; and I wondered whether, if Lilla could know my story and
dreams as well as I knew and guessed hers, she
would not look on me with the same kind of wondering pity wherewith I regarded her. And now,
behold, another bond of companionship and union!
Lilla had found for me my lost love: lo, I have
found her lost father! See, Lilla, there he is—
that broken-down, ridiculous reprobate yonder,
that billiard-room loafer, that ruined rattlepate
wretch in the black wig, who is stamping up and
down the room, blaspheming as he goes!

"Mr. Lyndon!"

"My dear young friend, a thousand pardons!
You recall me to myself, and remind me that I
am not playing the host to perfection. I *am*, I

fear, a little egotistic sometimes; but what would
you have of a man who has had to contend against
the world and his wife—his own wife, Temple;
not the world's, mind—for so many years? Ad-
versity, Temple, is the parent of egotism. Pardon
my distraction."

"I was not thinking of that; I was going to
ask a question."

"Propound. I reserve to myself the right of
not answering, should the answer tend to crimi-
nate me. In a moral point of view, Temple, it
would not be easy for me to give any answer re-
lating to my own personal history which would
not tend a little that way. But go on, youth of
the gloomy brow."

"Only this. What about your wife? You
said you were married."

"Did I admit so much? My old weakness—
too much confidence and candour. No matter.
You ask me what about my wife? Give you my
word, Temple, I don't know; I don't really. I
have been away so long, knocking about the plains
of windy Troy, that I positively don't know where
to find my Penelope now that I have come back."

"Should you like to?"

"O dear, no—not in the least. I couldn't think of it; she's doubtless very happy, and I should grieve to disturb her: or perhaps she is not very happy, and then the sight of her would disturb me. No, Temple; a man of refined taste shrinks from unidealising—if you will allow me to use such a word—from unidealising the poetic perfectness of married life by too much of vulgar intercourse with its prosy details."

"Still, as she is your wife—"

"Just so; there it is, you see. If she were not, then it would be quite a different thing: but she is my wife, and I know it to my cost. I paid a heavy debt for the sweet privilege of calling her so, and I am not ardent for any more of her mild society. You look horrified, I perceive. Frankly, I don't care."

"She may be poor and lonely—"

"My good fellow, am not *I* poor and lonely? Could anyone be poorer than I was the other day, and shall be soon again, no doubt? Am I not lonely, or worse than lonely, in having no companionship but that of a silly and moping young moralist like you? Do you think adding two poor people together produces wealth? Put to-

gether cipher and cipher, and see how much
better off you are for the result. Besides, have
I not told you I know nothing, absolutely nothing,
of her whereabouts?"

"But suppose—"

"I don't want to suppose: I decline to suppose. I tell you, Temple, I can't live on pap;
some men can, I believe; I can't. Food for babes
does not nourish me. I lived on it long enough,
and you see the result. If there is anything in
life I utterly detest, it is puling, meek, mawkish
goodness. I rage at it; it sets me mad. I long
to tear and tatter it."

"But your child—your daughter?"

"Did I tell you I had a daughter? Really,
you find me in a strangely-confiding mood to-
night. Well, I have a daughter; at least, I
know I had, and I believe I still have. What
then?"

"Only one might have thought—"

"Yes, one might, no doubt. One might have
thought that the father's heart would melt; that
he would burst into sobs, and exclaim, in broken
accents, 'My angel chee-ild!'—that he would
weep on the neck of the good person who had

appealed to his paternal feelings, and become a respectable member of society. In the domestic melodrama, Temple, from which I perceive already your principal ideas of life are drawn—what's the price of the gallery-seats in the Victoria?—that sort of thing does, I believe, familiarly occur. But this, Temple, is real life; and we are not on the stage of the Victoria. I make no doubt my daughter's a very well-brought-up and proper young woman, who would look with horror on such a reprobate as I am; and I cannot say that the voice of Nature shrieks very powerfully or plaintively in my ears. No, Temple, it won't do."

"Then have you really no care for anything?"

"Yes!" he answered in vehement and fierce tones—I had long been expecting an outburst of passion—"for money and for freedom! For money to spend, and for freedom to spend it in! Give me these—and I *will* have them, wherever I get them—and I can enjoy everything that life gives for enjoyment, from moonbeams and music up to absinthe and madness. But I will have money, and I will be free! I will, I will! I don't care who or what comes between me and my way of life; I sweep it out of my road and go on. Don't talk to me of nature and domestic affections, and drivel of that kind; I don't want them—I've had enough of them to last my time. Hate is much more in my line than love. I came to London for the double purpose of screwing money out of my thrice-accursed brother, and disgracing myself and him at the same time; and I will do it too! I would have done it before now, had not that fool of a woman sent me this money, which I mean to enjoy before I go to work. Pleasure first, business afterwards with me. Go to the devil with your talk about my wife and my chee-ild! What is it to you? Are you sent as an emissary here from Tommy Goodboy? If you are, go back to him and tell him what my answer is: tell him I'll make his respectability blush yet, if I cannot make his heart of pumice-stone feel."

"I never spoke a word to Mr. Lyndon in my life."

"Then perhaps you are an emissary from my wife. If you are, go back and tell her the best thing she can do is to leave me to myself."

"Listen to me, Mr. Lyndon, and don't waste on me all these rhapsodies and ravings. Keep them for somebody on whom they might produce some desirable effect. I assure you they move me only to sincere pity and contempt. I never knew until twenty minutes ago who you were, and I never cared. I spoke to you on no one's behalf, at no one's suggestion. I spoke to you only because I thought it hardly possible you could be wholly degraded below the feelings of average manhood. I find I was mistaken. That is enough. I leave you, and only hope we may not meet any more."

He threw himself into a chair, leaned back, and burst into a peal of mellow laughter. If I know anything of reality as distinguished from acting—and I ought—this was no affectation or sham, but genuine, honest, hearty, irrepressible laughter. He rolled about in his chair, and stamped his feet, and shook his shoulders like a pigmy Sam Johnson in a fit of unconquerable mirth.

I stood up, angry, and ashamed of being angry—thinking what a great deal I would give, if I had it, to feel myself at liberty to kick him; and all the time considering whether I could in any possible way serve poor Lilla's interests by keeping on good terms with him.

"I protest, Temple," he said at last, when he was able to speak from very laughing, "you do delight me. As good as a play? Man, you're worth a whole season of broad comedy! To look at the expression of your face that time, to watch your gesture, to hear the earnest eloquence of your language, was the finest treat any man with a rich sense of humour could possibly have. You are the most delightful of young men—"

"And you are the most scandalous of old reprobates."

" Coarse, Temple, coarse, and not half so fervent as your graver style. But I see you are waxing wroth at being laughed at. Well, I daresay no one likes being laughed at, and of course the more ridiculous he is, the less he likes being treated as such: and I really don't want to offend you; so let us consider the subject as dropped. Take a little more brandy? No? What, you are not going? Positively offended! Well, of all the idiots it has ever been my fortune to meet, you are the most conspicuous. Get out! Go to all the devils! Confound you, I am a gentleman, and not a Christy's Minstrel like you! Insult a gentleman! By Jove, what's the world coming to!"

All these concluding sentences were rattled at my ears as I was descending the stairs. Until I had fairly quitted the house I could hear him swearing and objurgating. Then, as I passed under the window, I found that he was having recourse to the piano to cool his wrath. I paused a moment out of curiosity. He was singing, to his own accompaniment, "I know that my Redeemer liveth."

I hurried away. The words, the sweet, pathetic, devotional tones, sounded in my ears like hideous blasphemy.

I walked slowly home, my mind occupied with the uncomfortable discovery I had made, and much perplexed to know whether there was anything I could or ought to say or do with regard to it. It clearly seemed that I had no right to inflict useless torture on Mrs. Lyndon or Lilla by telling them anything about my knowledge of this wretched man. From what he had over and over again told me, it was certain that he had come to London for the purpose of shaming his brother into supplying him with new funds, and it was evident that there was no extravagant escapade or exposure of which the little wretch would not be capable. On the whole, then, it seemed to me that the best thing I could do would be to see Mr. Lyndon at once, and put him on his guard. Mr. Lyndon too might, like a sensible man of the world, feel inclined to buy-off his disreputable brother even for Lilla's sake—to settle on him some pension on condition of his living out of England or out of Europe; and, disagreeable as the task would be, I would willingly undertake the work of negotiation and arrangement in order to ward-off vexation and shame from these two poor women, who had been so kind to me. Yes, that was the best thing to do, and there was no time to be lost, as Mr. Lyndon would be leaving town immediately. My mind was made up. Little as I cared to obtrude myself on Lilla's uncle, I determined to see him, in this cause, next day.

END OF VOL. I.

LONDON:

ROBSON AND SONS, PRINTERS, PANCRAS ROAD, N.W.

www.ingramcontent.com/pod-product-compliance
Lightning Source LLC
Chambersburg PA
CBHW060611030726
47498CB00005B/1638